COMING FOR YOU

Dirty, Dark, & Deadly #3

COMING FOR YOU

Dirty, Dark, & Deadly #3

J. A. HUSS

Edited by RJ Locksley
Cover Photo: Scott Hoover
Cover Model: Nick Ayler
Formatted by Tianne Samson with E.M. Tippetts Book Designs

E.M.
TIPPETTS
BOOK DESIGNS

ISBN-978-1-936413-77-5

Books By
JA HUSS

Losing Francesca

Science Fiction Series
Clutch
Fledge
Flight
Range
The Magpie Bridge
Return

Rook and Ronin Books
TRAGIC
MANIC
PANIC

Rook and Ronin Spinoffs
SLACK: A Day in the Life of Ford Aston
TAUT: The Ford Book
FORD: Slack/Taut Bundle
BOMB: A Day in the Life of Spencer Shrike
GUNS The Spencer Book

Dirty, Dark, and Deadly
Come
Come Back
Coming for You
James and Harper: Come/Come Back Bundle

Social Media

Follow
Like
Block
Status
Profile
Home

About This Book

James, Harper, and Sasha are products of their environment. Born into a secret organization that runs a global shadow government, and taught to kill since they were small, they find themselves both indispensable and expendable to all the people they used to trust.

Twenty-eight year old James Fenici has been an assassin since he was sixteen. He's amassed debts and favors from countless Company brothers and participated in hundreds of Company jobs. But there are not enough favors in the world to clear his debt and make him worthy of the only girl he's ever wanted.

Eighteen year old Harper Tate is the girl who doesn't exist. Born and raised on a megayacht in a tropical paradise, she was destined to be a secret until now. No history, no records, and manipulated into having no opinions or ambition of her own, Harper is suddenly presented with more choices than she can handle.

Thirteen year old Sasha Cherlin is the girl who knows everything and understands nothing at all. Her future is filled with vengeance and death, but her dreams are filled with hope and a promise. A promise who no longer wants her.

The game is on, the pieces are in place, and the players have everything to lose. But who can you trust when everyone's a traitor?

PART ONE

PROLOGUE

Sasha

Last Christmas Eve

I see him, but he doesn't see me.

I'm practicing for the future. That's how hunters work. You gotta be sneaky.

His friend, who I have seen before—but who ignores me like I'm dust—goes into the back room to meet my dad. It's a gun run, so I don't pay any attention to him. But this guy, the guy who looks like he *could* be a hunter, but whom I've never seen before, which makes it unlikely (though not impossible), that he *is* a hunter, stops to look at stuff after his friend tells him to wait.

He picks up a knife.

"That knife sucks," I say from my seat across the aisle. "I wouldn't buy that one."

He checks the brand, then the blade. "Yeah, this is crap." He puts it in the basket and I make my move.

I set my *Little House* book down and walk over to him. "Wanna see the good ones?" I ask. He turns and looks surprised that I got so close without him hearing me.

I'm good at being sneaky.

I show him the good knives and he looks at me like I'm weird. They all look at me like that once I let them into my world. They know I'm different. This guy—Ford, he says his name is—he knows I'm different. He jokes with me about grownup stuff. He laughs and listens to me when I help him shop for his mom and girl-who-is-a-friend. I gift-wrap his two presents, and while I do that, I realize something.

I've known almost from the moment he walked in that he's a good guy.

His friend peeks out of the back room and tells Ford to leave. Things are getting complicated. My stomach does a little turn at that word. I don't like it. I like things to be simple. Complicated is bad. I switch my frown to a smile before Ford catches it. "You have time for me to gift-wrap your knife."

"It's for me, Sasha. It doesn't need to be gift-wrapped."

"It's like a present to yourself, Ford. Just go with it."

He laughs. I keep my back to him and concentrate on my gift-wrapping as he asks why I'm working today.

Why am I working today?

Buddy, I think to myself, *you would not believe me if I told you.* I reach in my pocket and palm the little hard drive I took from my dad last night. He was drunk. My dad hardly ever gets drunk. And as much as I'd like to believe my Christmas Eve is going to end up with me sleeping soundly at my grandparents' ranch tonight, I'm pretty sure that's not what's happening today.

When the hunters show up, bad things happen.

I pull the flash drive out of my pocket and slip it inside Ford's knife box. When he opens this tomorrow, he'll find an old battered piece of plastic covered in stickers. If he plugs the drive into his computer, he'll see photographs. All my best moments in my short life.

And maybe that's the end of it. Maybe he tucks it inside a drawer somewhere, laughing at the little girl up in Wyoming who got attached. Maybe he never thinks of it, or me, again.

I can only hope.

But I don't think that's what's gonna happen.

I think that by the time this is all over, he might wish he never met me.

ONE

Sasha - Present Day

Some people look peaceful when they sleep.

James Fenici is not one of them.

He doesn't talk, or thrash wildly from nightmares. Only stupid people do that. Weak people.

James Fenici is not weak. He's a lot of things, but he's not weak.

No. James has this little twitch. It's almost not noticeable, and it only affects the one eye. But it's there. I've been watching him for about an hour. I've been on a private plane twice now—once on my way to Vegas, and this time, on my way home from California. But let me tell you something. They are pretty fucking boring.

Fracking. Fudging. Flucking. I should not swear in my thoughts. James hates it when I swear and if I swear in my thoughts, I'll swear in real life.

But fuck it. This plane ride sucks. There are no drinks because Harrison was too busy fishing me out of the ocean after James shot me to stock up the cooler.

Yeah. This stupid plane has a cooler. Like something you put ice in. Not like a refrigerator that even our stupid nineteen seventy-eight RV had back when I was a kid. A cooler. I'm not impressed.

So no soda. Not even a fracking, fudging, flucking bag of pretzels.

God, I'm so hungry.

"James?"

He's across the aisle from me, but that's like two feet away tops. I kick him when he doesn't answer.

"James?"

"Kick me again, and I'll break all your toes," he says without opening his eyes.

"I'm *so* hungry."

He cracks one eye open. "Do I look like a vending machine? I told you, we'll stop in Burlington after we get the truck." He closes the one eye like this matter is settled.

"How far away is Burlington?"

"Go ask Harrison."

And that's it. I watch him for a few minutes to see if he'll apologize for not having food. But he doesn't. He's asleep again because there's that twitch.

I don't want to ask Harrison. He'll say something with coordinates that make no sense without a map. If it was light I could look out the window and at least see if we passed the mountains yet. Burlington is on the prairie.

I slump down in my seat and pout. I know that's very childish and I should man up and stop doing it. But I'm not a man and I'm still a child. So hey, might as well enjoy it while I can.

I think of Nick instead.

I can't believe he never told Harper about me. Is that weird? She didn't even know I was his promise. That's not weird. I don't think, anyway. Promises are supposed to be secret. I shouldn't know Nick and I are promised. But he told me last year when he started coming to see me in Wyoming.

Well, he came to see my dad. But he took an interest in me and it was very hard for me not to take an interest back because Nick Tate is what girls call *hot.*

He and Harper have some similarities, obviously, since they are twins. But Nick is taller than Harper. He's got nice muscles for a boy of only eighteen. Not like James. James has man muscles.

He's a big guy compared to Nick. But Nick is quicker than James. Harper is quicker than James too. I saw her fight a little while we were together.

Nick is smart too. He knows so many things. He knows secrets for one. Secrets that even James doesn't know.

Hell, even I know secrets that James doesn't know.

But if I thought that gave me an advantage, I'd be wrong because there's more to James than just... *James.*

Of course, there's the little matter of Number One too. He tried to kill Harper. And I don't know what to make of all this. Or of James' sister, Nicola. Or the Admiral. Or Nick for that matter.

Who should I trust?

So far it's just James. But once I see Nick, I'll have to make a choice. Because you can't be loyal to two people at once.

Can you?

Harrison yells from the cockpit. "We're getting ready to land, you guys. Buckle up."

James lowers his feet off the seat across from him and sits up straight. Has he been awake this whole time? Shit, I stopped watching him. Did he see me thinking?

I don't like to think about secrets in front of James. It's not like he reads minds or anything, but he's got instincts. He reads faces. And body language. And even voices.

I know because my father taught me how to do it too. But the thing about instincts is that you have to use them in real life to make them second nature.

I have never done a job. Aside from killing those four men who came to blow up my grandparents' ranch, I've never done anything exciting. All the teaching in the world is useless without experience.

James has experience. James has killed hundreds of people. He's overthrown governments. He's worked in conditions I can't even imagine. And he was a prisoner of war down in Honduras once.

I've heard that story enough times to recite it in my sleep from people more important than him. Back in the desert he told Harper and me that he was running a shadow government down in San Pedro Sula, but that wasn't his first time in Honduras. No.

The first time was when he was captured.

I know what happened to him down there. Both times. I chance a look over at my new partner and smile.

"What's on your mind, Smurf?"

Shit.

"I'm so, so, so, so hungry." He stares at me and I can't help myself. I squirm.

"Burlington has a McDonalds. We'll get some breakfast there."

I would die for McDonalds right now. "And then what are we gonna do?"

The plane drops the landing gear with a thud and this gives James the opportunity to ignore my question.

I don't like when he ignores my questions. Because that means I won't like the answer he's not giving me.

"We're partners, right?" I ask him, suddenly feeling needy.

He turns back to me with a smile. I love it when he smiles. Because as far as I can tell, the smiles are never fake. "Till death do us part, midget."

I smile back. I really do like James. I'm just not sure I can *trust* James.

Because as far as I've been able to tell, Tet is in charge in all the situations that count. The most notable was back at Merc's house in the desert when he told me he might have a plan. The second time was after Harper was drugged by One. I'm still not one hundred percent sure of who was actually in charge that first time. But the guy who told me he was going to shoot me in the chest was definitely Tet.

And even though I think James is on the up and up, I have a hard time understanding how he can live two lives at the same time.

Everyone in the Company—and I do mean *everyone*—knows that James Fenici is a twisted dude. You need him to kill his brother? No problem. Just tell Tet. You need him to kill a trainer's kid? No problem. Just tell Tet. You need him to trail your daughter and lead everyone on a wild chase to take the heat off your son? No problem. Just tell Tet.

But the problem with James and Tet doubles when you realize you can't have one without the other. They are not two separate personalities.

They really are the same guy.

I think that makes James/Tet more insane than if he was one of those crazy people with split personality disorder. Because at least if they were two people you could sorta count on them.

For instance, when the Admiral texted James and told him to come out to Colorado and "pick me up" what he really expected was for Tet to come out to Colorado to "pick me off".

Nick told me the night before James showed up. He said, *If you see him first, he's James and you should give him a chance. If he shows up as Tet, you'll never know he was there.*

Is it fucked up that Nick didn't just tell me to get the hell out of there?

I'm not sure.

But Tet wasn't around when that text from the Admiral to come "pick me up" came in. James was. And James was busy with Harper, so he didn't need Tet.

See, the Admiral, for all his uppity smugness, really has no clue how James/Tet operates. I suppose that's why he instructed me to kill James that day. It was a two birds kind of thing.

I'm pulled out of my thoughts when the plane touches down, bounces once, then again, and we roll the rest of the way towards the small airport surrounded by cornfields on three sides.

When we come to a stop James stands up and stretches his arms above his head and touches the top of the cabin, pressing his hands flat against the curved plastic. "I'm starved too, McSmurf. And I need coffee." He says that with a smile.

God, I love that smile. I might not like Tet all that much, and James is not one of those nurturing people like my dad was. But when he smiles at me like that, I absolutely love him.

TWO

James

I watch the Smurf watch me through the smallest crack of an eye during our plane ride.

She's making me nervous. She's not asleep, but she thinks I am. She's watching me, but she has no idea I'm watching her.

Jesus fucking Christ. I have no idea what I'm doing. I know things they don't think I know. But I'm not even sure what to do with some of that information.

And I have no idea what Sasha is doing. I know she's operating on someone's orders. I'm just not sure who's orders they are. The Admiral? She definitely was. But now? Not sure. Nick? Don't know about that either.

Merc? Now that's the real mystery. The one that matters most right now because he's the first person we're gonna see.

And Nick. I haven't seen him in a long time, but Merc has. He knows a lot about me. Maybe more than he should. Definitely more than he should.

And so this is the test. Who works for who is a question I've had no solid answer to for a very long time. But pretty soon all the players will be present and I can sort it out.

But pretty soon is not now, so I need to just let it go. I'm moving forward on trust alone. I have to trust her. It's my only option.

I think about Harper instead and that makes my chest hurt in a way that's new to me. When I saw her lying on the floor in her old apartment—fuck. I stopped breathing. It had to have been no more than two, three seconds. But it felt like eternity. Slow mo, right? They say that in emergencies, time changes. And I believe it. I've felt that a lot over the years. When reality is so in your face. When death is right there—all you gotta do is reach out and he'll pull you across that thin veil and make it all end, once and for all.

I've been there so many times. But the first time is the one you never forget.

Honduras. Twelve years ago. James Fenici, barely Six, not yet Tet. Already fucked up.

Even now when I close my eyes, I hear the spray of bullets. My hands were shaking so bad I couldn't even load my fucking rifle. And when I finally shot my first gang member down in the fucked up place they call San Pedro Sula, I missed. The first bullet skimmed past his temple, just enough to ruin his eye, and give me a nice visual burned into my memory. Still, to this day.

I never even got a chance to fire a second shot and finish the job, because I was caught and the guy who was forever called Mistake Number One in my head lived.

But I'm sure he looked in the mirror every day and wished he hadn't. I'm sure he looked in the mirror every day and told himself he lived for one thing only. To make James Fenici pay.

I was in custody long enough to be tortured by him personally after he recovered. They burned me. They choked me. Hell, they hanged me once. Not enough to break my neck, obviously, just enough that I had to stand on my tiptoes for hours… days, sometimes.

They say the reason I'm so dangerous now is because I never gave up then. And I guess that's true. I don't. I figure fuck this goddamned world. It's got nothing I can't take. All I gotta do is become Tet when the time starts to slow down and he steps right in. He's got no problem blowing heads off and Tet does not miss.

If you're gonna kill someone, you finish the job or die trying.

Because it's *no gusta* hanging around to get caught or having to go back and try it again. Take it from me. I know. I got caught and I went back to finish the job of taking over the city they call *Murder Capital of the World*. It was like combining the worst moment of my life with a weird sensation of coming home.

I think that's when Tet really started to take an interest in my jobs. I don't consider Southern California home anymore, not since I left there when I was sixteen. But thinking of Honduras as home back then? That was a new level of fucked up, even for me.

It took me years to understand that I was different. When One came to rescue me from the Honduran gangs, I had an inkling. His third name is Shroom because his calling-card poison is amatoxin. Poison mushrooms. We get assigned a poison to use when we need to kill people for personal reasons. Mine's the toxin found in the blue ring octopus. Classic James Bond kinda shit.

Tet the toxin is a blockbuster movie way to die, for sure.

But Tet the dude? He's definitely more of a Goldfinger kinda character.

I don't know whose idea it was to give us three names, but I took that shit seriously because when your job requires you to interact with some of the biggest scumbags on Earth, you gotta keep it in perspective.

Tet.

I can feel him inside me. He tips his hat in greeting. He's relaxed right now. His version of winding down at the beach. But that's because I'm with the kid and I think Harper is safe for now.

Fucking Harper. I miss her more than I'd like to admit because there's just no telling how all this shit will play out. I have no idea who is on my side inside the Company or who is actively working against me. They might be using her to get to me. They might be using me to get to her. Hell, anything is possible at this point. I don't know if a single person can say they understand their loyalties these days.

It's a sketchy world at the best of times, but the Company has seen the last of the best of times. Ever since Harper and Nick took off with that file, everyone's been on edge.

What's on the file? Only one person knows that for sure. The person who made it.

And he's dead.

I don't know a lot about it, but I do know they can't access it. Before Nick took it, they had every expert on the planet trying to get past the firewall.

That's one reason they brought in Merc. And fuck—what good luck for them that the guy was a professional mercenary. He was working private security when I was sent to Europe to recruit him. He was not interested and it was dropped. But we got to be friends over the years. He'd call me. I'd help. I'd call him. He'd help. Debts, man. Debts make the world go round.

And then one day... a call came in to his home phone while he was busy and I was minding the shop. And I listened to that message.

And who do you think that call was from?

Ford fucking Aston.

Turns out Merc has a similar *quid pro quo* arrangement with Aston, and this call was a cash-in for a debt Merc owed him.

It was a small identity theft request. But that wasn't the interesting part. The interesting part was when Ford said, *I'd do it myself, but I need to keep my distance.*

Which told me two things. Ford was not above fucking with people's lives. And he had skills in his own right. Both of which might come in handy for me.

Tet took over from there. Merc came back from that job, it was a total fuckup, and as soon as he walked in the door, the message was playing.

I'm not sure if he knew about Tet before he came home that night, but he sure the fuck knew of him by the time we were done.

Tet blackmailed him. Either he does the job I need him for, or I call Ford back and get him involved.

And for some reason, Merc is loyal to that asshole in a suit. He caved. I gave him a number, Seven, and a calling card. If your name is already Merc, it only makes sense to become mercury.

As far as I know, Merc kills whoever he wants, whenever he wants, and he has never actually bothered to poison someone with mercury.

Which is why the Company started thinking up ways to get rid of him once his usefulness wore off. He's not exactly a team player.

Hence the 'accident' up in Wyoming last Christmas.

The Admiral was not happy about that fuckup. I know that for a fact because I was sent to eliminate the assassin who botched the job when both Merc and Sasha showed up alive the next day.

Of course, this is all hindsight shit. I didn't know what the fuck was happening last year. All I knew was I was being sent to kill people who were supposed to be on our side.

No one knows who to trust these days.

We're all guilty. We're all killers, even if we're not all numbered assassins. We're all wary of each other.

Because that file has been floating around for more than a year now. And from what they say, that file has enough dirt on it to cut the entire Company off at the knees.

I don't get this file. I have no idea what's on it. I think just your basic who's who kind of info. Which means I'm in there. My family's in there. We're all in there, I guess. But who gives a fuck? Really, if some investigative reporter gets a hold of it and flashes that info for everyone to see, who would believe it? It's like a very bad Dan Brown conspiracy book. This shit is so twisted, and the people involved so high up, and the accusations about what we're doing so outlandish no one would even believe it. People just ignore shit that's too big. You tell them small things—like we busted a terror cell in Colorado but the guy's in custody, or there was a helicopter crash in Afghanistan and ten Navy SEALs died—and they're OK with that. People can process that shit.

But when you get a guy who climbs the White House fence so he can get on TV and try and tell people what we're doing by naming names… nope. That's crazy talk. People don't process the big shit well at all.

A plane 'disappears' over the Indian Ocean and everyone goes, huh? Wonder what happened.

A plane goes missing. Hundreds of people. Missing.

No one bats an eye.

So who gives a fuck about this file? That's what I don't understand. It's big shit. It's a list of global criminals masquerading as lawmakers and politicians. But there's so many people on it—so many government agencies, charities, movie stars, and moms and pops—it's gotta be bullshit. I mean, come on. How could this shadow world exist right under everyone's nose?

So I can give a fuck about this file.

But that was before One killed Harper to get it back. Now that file is all I think about. And my sister. He mentioned my sister. He said she was in on the plan. And holy motherfuck. I can totally see that. I can totally fucking see that. It's like all these little bits and pieces of my life and memory are all coming back to me.

But that file. It's all wrong how it went down.

Nick steals the file, gives it to Harper, tells her to poison a ship full of Company elite, and then sends her away. But he only gives her the outward appearance of escaping. He only gives her just enough cover to make her *think* she's getting away.

I'm debriefed, along with the rest of the remaining assassins—but told not to approach. No one is to approach her because she's dangerous.

Yeah, Harper has some moves, but Harper is not dangerous. She's like a little kitten with those little kitten claws. She can hurt you, but she's a *kitten*.

So everyone gives her a wide berth. Meanwhile Tony's number comes up and he's next on my list. At the same time, Ford calls in a favor to Merc, who calls in a favor to me, requesting that my crazy brother also be eliminated.

So yeah, I did it.

Well—I take a deep breath and crack an eye to see if Sasha noticed, but she's deep in thought too—I didn't do it. Tet did it. Tet did it and then Tet didn't move to the back of the bus, so to speak. Tet decided to take the front seat, in fact. And that made me fail the psych evaluation.

Which got me sent to the beach to unwind.

And then One appeared with a video of my sister, Nicola. And she had black eyes and she asked me to help her. And One told me to get that file because I had a debt to pay.

I sigh again.

They played me. They knew Harper was a weakness. I'd stayed clear of her except on her birthdays. Still, certain people knew I went to see her every Six Day. They knew she interacted with me the day we turned Six. They figured—correctly, I might add—that I could tame her.

But I love her. I want her. I know she's not my promise. I understand this and it killed me to lie to her while we were together. But I want her now. She's mine.

And no one is going to take her away.

No one.

THREE

James

When Harrison yells back that we're finally landing, I get up and stretch. I shoot the Smurf a smile that says it's all good and make small talk about food, then I sit back down to wait for the plane to stop.

When we get off, I stop to shake Harrison's hand. "You ever need anything, Harrison, I'm your man."

He smiles but I can tell all he's thinking about is how he hopes he never needs the kind of services I offer.

"Thanks, Harrison," Sasha says, giving him a hug. He squeezes her back, a little too hard maybe because she puts a hand to her chest where my bullet slammed into her last night, and he pulls away.

"Sorry, Sasha," he says in his kind voice. "Be careful," he adds, as he pats her on the back. And then he looks at me like I am scum.

"She'll be OK, I promise."

"I'll be fine, Harrison. Don't worry about me." She points to the parking lot, which is sorta visible from where we're at. "Hey, there's your truck, James!" And then she's off. Running like a kid.

"Tet… James… whoever the fuck you are. Don't drag this kid down with you, man. It's not right. You can leave her here. My wife and I don't have any kids. We can always use the company."

My eyes squint down as I stare at him. I have never really looked at Harrison before. He's not quite middle age. His hair is still dark, his build still decent for a guy who sits for his job. His eyes are too kind to be part of my world. And I bet he's got a nice home here in this town. Some no-nonsense bungalow that could be anywhere.

But he's out of his fucking mind if he thinks he's getting my Smurf.

"I mean, just until you figure shit out, not for good. Just for a little while. To keep her safe."

I don't care for what he's insinuating. "She's safest with me, Harrison."

"You shot her in the chest, Tet. That's not normal. That's just fucking wrong."

I grit my teeth and clench my fist. He needs to stop or I might just lose my temper. "I did what I had to do to save her fucking life. Now, if you don't mind, we've got people to meet. I hope we're still good after this, but if not, just ignore my next call and you'll never hear from me again."

And then I turn my back and walk away.

Sasha is sitting on the hood of the black Toyota Tundra pickup. "I can't believe your truck is still here," she laughs.

I shoot her a grin. "Why wouldn't it be? It's only been a few days."

"I know," she says excitedly, jumping down and walking over to the passenger side door. I click the lock on the key chain and the lights blink once. We get in at the same time and slam the doors closed. "But it feels like a lifetime, doesn't it?"

"It does." It really fucking does. I start the truck and take a deep breath.

"You miss her already?"

"Yeah," I say, putting the truck in gear. "Dropping her off with the Admiral is a huge risk."

"Do you think he'll hurt her?" Sasha asks, the worry coming through in her voice.

"Nah. That's not what I'm worried about. Now buckle up, it's the law."

She snorts at that, but it serves its purpose. She drops the line of questioning.

I'm worried about him hurting her, sure. He's not looking out for her. Not the way he is Nick. He left her at the beach for a year. Fighting the panic and barely surviving. They *both* left her at the beach for a year.

And that file she had. No. Something is wrong about that file. If One has it, why haven't we been called back?

I mean I know why *I* haven't. I'm crazy and I'm pretty sure the next hit will be on my head.

But the Company has always been disciplined. We're a military faction, albeit a covert black-ops one. We have rules and traditions. We have… protocols.

None of those seem to matter these days.

And it all leads back to the fucking Admiral. Why does he want her back now? I didn't lie to Harper when I told her I haven't talked to him in a long time. But I was not very forthcoming, either. Because he contacts me regularly with the phones. Almost everywhere I go, I find a phone. He always knows where I am. I've never hidden from him. So when I found the phone in my truck before I found Sasha, it was no big deal.

But maybe it is a big deal?

He asked me to bring her home *before* he got news of the file. So what was he thinking?

He wants to turn her against you, James, Tet says in my head. *He wants to get her alone and turn her against you.*

But why?

Because he set you up, James.

If there's one person on this earth who knows me, it's the Admiral. If there's one person on this earth who knows what's wrong with me, it's him. And if there's one person on the earth who can turn her against me, it's him.

I drive the truck across the freeway and hit the McDonalds where we pick up breakfast, then head north on one of the side roads. I am on edge the whole time Sasha is eating, just waiting for the questions to start. But she finishes her food, looks out the window at the farmhouses passing by, and then drops off to sleep.

A few hours later, when we get to the next big small town, I start heading west. The drive is quiet and uneventful. Just a two-lane highway that gives me way too much time to think.

I go west, zig-zagging my way through the back roads of Colorado, until hours later we reach I-25.

I turn north, staring at the road signs as they count down the miles to Fort Collins and when that exit appears, I take the off-ramp and drive into the town. It's still pretty quiet in downtown even though it's lunchtime. There's a university campus here, but I guess most of the students goes home for the summer. I spot the tattoo shop first and then a little farther down, the bike shop.

There's a ton of people outside the bike shop. Spencer Shrike himself, in fact. I turn my head just in case he sees me and then hang a left at the next street, and then a right another block down.

When the red roof of the condo building comes into view I almost turn around. But I need to see it. I pull up to the curb and put the truck in park, leaving the engine running.

Sasha is still asleep, so I exit the truck quietly and push the door closed until I hear the click. I don't want to tell Sasha why I'm here. I don't want to tell anyone why I'm here.

I walk up to the footpath security gate and then grab the spear-shaped finials of the iron bars and jump up, swinging my leg over and landing on the other side with a soft thud.

I look behind me to see if anyone is paying attention, but it's clear. So I walk to the side door of the building and open it, take the stairs down, and push open the heavy door that leads to the garage.

This is where Veronica got shot. I look over to my right. That spot was where she fell. Where Ford tied off her arm and saved her life.

Did I shoot her?

I actually don't know if it was me or…

My eyes wander until I find a dark stain in the middle of the garage.

Tony.

I walk over to the stain. There's no cars in here, so I can only assume they never finished the construction. When I found this building the builder ran out of money and it was just sitting half empty. Looks like that hasn't changed.

I kneel down next to the stain and call it like it is. The stain of my brother's brains as his head splattered from the force and velocity of my bullet.

I look behind me and imagine Ashleigh and Kate. My perfect little niece. I never knew Ash. I could give a fuck about that girl. But she's the mother of my niece and that means something. She's family. And I don't have much family.

I look back at what's left of Tony's mark in this world. "I'm sorry," I tell him. "I swear to God, I'm sorry. I just need to make this end. And it's not your fault you were crazy. It's not my fault I'm crazy. They did this to us and if I let you take Kate, they'd do it to her too."

I swallow hard and stand up, taking in a long breath of air.

"I'm gonna end it all, one way or another."

I look up and wait. For some kind of signal. Or feeling of forgiveness. Or something.

But that's Hollywood movie bullshit. I only deal in reality. And in reality, there's no such thing as forgiveness. There's no such thing as redemption. And there's no such thing as justice.

There's only revenge.

I nod at the stain and turn, going back the way I came. When I get to the gate, I open it instead of jumping over since I'm on the inside now. And then I walk back to the running truck where Sasha still sleeps with her face pressed up against the cool window.

I put the truck in gear and watch a few bikers go by in a roar of power a block down.

I look back at Sasha and consider Harrison's offer. He'd never be able to control this kid. Because she's not a kid, she's a killer. But…

I look down the street, past the courthouse and let my eyes fall on the Catholic school across the street from the city buildings.

… but Ford lives here. Two miles away, across from a huge park. The park has a pool. And an ancient trolley that rides down the middle of his goddamned street. His life right now is something out of a postcard.

Sasha loves Ford. Ford would take her, I know he would.

I stop at the red light and just stare at the school, trying to picture Sasha happy and normal.

I want that for her, I do. But… I need her too much to let her go.

The next time I look up, the light is green so I make a left, back towards the freeway. Where I will take Sasha to the last place on earth she wants to be.

That's right, James. You're an asshole. You have a chance to give her a new family, but no. You deny her that opportunity so she can play her part in your sick plan that will never work.

But the funny thing is… Tet isn't concerned with any of those messy feelings. And so I let James slip away as the road passes by. James zones out and Tet takes over.

After all, he's the one who gets things done.

He's the one who keeps us alive.

And right now, staying alive is the only thing that matters.

Until it's time to kill.

FOUR

Sasha

When James gets out of the truck I watch him from the crack of my eyelids. I know where we're at. Fort Collins. Ford worked here last year. His friends live here. If I got out of this truck right now and went back to that bike shop, I could find him.

But James…

I'm worried about him. I wait until he's out of sight and then I follow him down to the garage. I peek through the door as he has some kind of internal struggle. I know what he did here. Nick told me.

He killed his brother.

And the first time I heard that I felt there was no way I could like James, let alone love him. But I was wrong.

When it looks like he's finished I trot silently back up the stairs, run down the path, and put myself back to sleep inside the truck.

When James comes back and we get back on the road, I know what he's thinking as we wait for the light. The light is green and he's still sitting there trying to come to terms with what he *needs* to do and what he *should* do.

He should take me to Ford and drop me off.

And I'm gonna be honest, a part of me really wants that. A part of me thinks if anyone can fix me—change me back into a little girl—then it's Ford.

But I heave a silent sigh of relief when he finally turns and takes us north, away from the town. And when we get to the freeway thirty minutes later and we're still going north, I have to come to terms with where we're actually going.

Cheyenne.

He's taking me home—except it's not my home anymore.

I have not been back to Cheyenne since last Christmas Eve when my father was killed. I ended up in the hospital and then my grandparents came and picked me up and took me back to their ranch in northern Wyoming.

Ford came to see me the next day on Christmas. He drove all the way from Denver, he said. Drove all night long. Almost eight hours.

And when he found me sitting in the bay window seat in my room, he sat down next to me and made his promise.

His hand is cold from driving in that piece-of-shit Bronco he showed up in. I pull away, but he squeezes—hard.

I look up into his soft brown eyes and shake my head, trying not to cry.

"Sasha," he says. "I swear to God, they will not get away with this. We will make this right."

"How?" I ask him, wiping my hand across my nose to stop the sniffling. "You don't have any idea who we're dealing with. You don't know anything. You're not even a hunter."

"You're right, I'm not. But I am a consultant. And my partner, Merc, he is a hunter. And he's still alive. I talked to him."

I clench my fists together so hard my fingernails dig into my skin. "He should be dead!" I scream that last part. "He should be dead, not my dad!"

There's a few moments of silence and I figure he's on the defensive now. He's not sure what to do with me. I count on that when I'm dealing with men. A small girl has very little power in a big man's world. But I do what I can by keeping them off guard.

I look up at him expecting sympathy, but I get a sneer instead.

"Don't play me, kid. I'm not in the fucking mood. I drove eight goddamned hours to be here and give you this." He holds opens his fist to reveal a flash drive.

Yesterday Ford came into my dad's gun shop at the antique mall with his friend Merc. And while Merc was buying guns, Ford bought some Christmas presents for his mom and friend.

The flash drive was my present to him.

Sorta.

The present was my last-ditch attempt to get rid of the flash drive before someone came looking for it.

I stifle a cry as I realize I might be the reason my father is dead right now. I reach for it but Ford closes his fist again and pulls away. "Not so fast."

I stare at him.

"What is this?"

I blink my eyes innocently.

"On first glance, it's a drive with photos on it. Of a girl and her father and all their crazy times together. But that's not what it is, is it?"

I say nothing.

"If people are looking for this, you better fucking say so. You understand? Because people are dead, Sasha."

"I know," I cry. "I know. But I swear I didn't know this would happen."

"So what's on here?" he asks.

"I don't know. But I'm afraid to keep it now. Yesterday morning I saw two guys who I know are supposed to be dead. They were standing outside the antique mall, smoking cigarettes. I knew… I just knew they were there looking for that drive. And I got scared and put it in with your gift-wrapped knife to get it away."

"How the fuck did you know I wouldn't hand it over to someone who shouldn't have it?"

"I just knew." I look up at Ford and silently plead with him to help me. "I just knew, Ford. You're the only good person I've met in a very long time. And now my dad is gone and I have no one."

He looks at my open door, then gets up and checks the hallway for my grandpa. My grandma can't climb stairs and my grandpa isn't much better. So they don't come up here much. But Ford closes the bedroom door just the same and walks back over to me, not taking a seat this time. "Sasha, I'm taking this with me and I'm giving it to Merc. He works for these people. And something is very wrong here. But I'm not the right guy to help you, OK? I'm not the right guy."

I realize I've been holding my breath.

"Merc is the one you need. So you're gonna stay up here in the middle of who-gives-a-fuckville and keep your head down and your eyes open. If you see anyone, Sasha—and I do mean anyone—you use this phone."

He hands it over. It's one of those cheap ones you can buy at Wal-Mart that all the hunters have to keep in touch without the Company knowing.

"There's only one number on there. You call Merc if you see anything and he'll tell you what to do. When I leave here I'll stop off at his place and we'll have a chat. Then he'll get in touch with you. But no matter what happens, Sasha"—Ford pauses to make sure I'm listening—"no matter what happens, you do not tell anyone about this drive and you do not tell anyone about me coming here today. Do you understand?"

I nod. "Yes, sir."

And like it or not. Ford was right. He's the wrong guy to handle this.

But so is Merc.

Because James… James is the only guy who can handle this.

FIVE

James

"Quit that. You're driving me nuts."

"What?" I ask as I chew on my thumbnail, wishing I could have a smoke. I ran out forty miles ago and there were no stops on the highway. And now that we're in Cheyenne, I'm nervous as all hell.

"Just stop for cigarettes, for Pete's sake. I'm the one who should be nervous. This is my home, not yours."

I look at her as we stop at the red light. "Why would you be nervous?"

"Well." She looks out the window. "We're going to the Roundhouse, right?"

That's the name of the antique mall her dad sold Company guns out of. "Yeah. You expecting something important to be there, Smurf?"

Because I am. And that's what's got me nervous.

"Not exactly."

I don't know what that means, but a horn honks behind me and I look up to find the light has turned green. I ease forward and then take the first right past the railroad tracks. The old-timey train station is on the right side of this road and on the left are historical warehouse buildings that have been re-purposed into antique stores.

The Roundhouse is massive and it's on a corner one street up.

Sasha lets out a deep breath.

Fuck. I hope to hell this is not a mistake. I pull the truck around the back of the building and park next to a giant green dumpster and cut the engine.

"Well," I say as we sit in silence for a moment. "Ready to go inside?"

I turn my head to look at her and she's got wide eyes. "Do I need to be ready for something?"

"You tell me."

"Have you been in here before?"

I shake my head at her. "Never. Never been to this town before, I told you that."

"I wasn't sure if that was true or not. It's seems unlikely that you never stopped by here for something."

"This depot isn't that old, Sasha. The gunrunner for the western guys used to be in Arizona."

"Oh." She nods and takes a deep breath. "That makes sense, I guess. We used to live out of the RV and just sell at gun shows."

We open our doors at the same time and get out of the truck. I point to the back door and we head that direction. When we get there I hurry a little to open it for her and she scoots inside without another word.

Please, I pray, *don't let this be a mistake.*

We enter into a back room and I have no idea where I'm going. Merc just said to park in back and go through the door.

I don't need to worry. The Smurf leads the way. There's aisle after aisle of tall industrial-sized shelving like you see in a big box store, but Sasha goes up two aisles, walks down one until we get to an intersection, and then makes a left. At the end of this aisle is another door. "Where we going?" I ask her as she heads for the door.

"My dad's booth," she says, cool as they come.

Of course. Whenever I come to the Roundhouse to meet

mercenaries, I always hit the dead father's booth first.

The door has a lock with one of those silver punch pads above the knob. Sasha punches in a code and sure enough, it opens.

I follow her through and we are in another storeroom. Only this one is filled with weapons.

I hear the tell-tale cock of a shotgun and I've got my Five-SeveN out and pointing at Merc's face before he can laugh.

"You dumbfuck." He puts his hands up and starts waving the gun around like an idiot. "Don't shoot me, bro! Don't shoot me, bro!"

I walk over and grab the gun from his hands. "It's don't *taze* me, you idiot. Not shoot me."

"Whatever," he says, taking out a smoke and handing me one. "Same shit." He pulls out a light and offers it to me. I suck on the cancer stick and let the nic run through my veins. Jesus. Never has a cigarette felt so good.

Merc lights his up too and then takes his own drag of relief. "So, what the fuck?" He's laughing and puffing at the same time. "You still have this runt with you? Jesus. You have more patience than me."

Sasha kicks him in the shin. "Asshole."

Merc bends over and rubs his leg like it hurts and then grabs Sasha by the waist, hoists her over his head, and he's about to body-slam her on a stack of boxes when I start to freak out.

"Dude!" I yell. "Do not fuck with my Smurf."

He flips her over, ignoring her screams, and then plops her down on the ground feet first.

"I'm kidding, you assholes. Jesus Christ. Lighten up. I'm the only one with a sense of humor here."

"OK, what's the plan?" I'm ready to get this show on the road.

"We're still waiting. Shouldn't be too long though."

"Then what?"

"Then"—he shrugs—"we play it by ear, I guess."

"Do you have the file or what?" Sasha barks from a safe distance.

"What file?" I ask, looking at her, then back to Merc. They stare each other down. "What. Fucking. File?"

Merc points his cigarette at Sasha. "I told you to keep your fucking mouth shut about that file."

"I have," she sneers back. "But I'm with him now," she says, pointing to me. "And I want him to know about it. So my silence is over." She pauses for a beat. "Do you have a problem with that?"

Damn. Assassin Smurf is back. I love Assassin Smurf. "What fucking file?" I ask again while Merc decides if he has a problem with that. Because of course, even if he did, it's too late now. Sasha has let me in.

Finally. After carting her midget ass all over the Wild West, I'm in.

Merc lets out a long breath and then does the little this-is-only-between-you-and-me gesture with his pointer finger. "We got the fucking file."

"Have had it the whole time, actually."

I look over at Sasha. "*You* had the file?"

She smiles. "No. I gave it to Ford and he gave it to Merc."

I look at Merc. "You had the fucking file? And you let me chase after Harper trying to get it? Does Nick know this shit?"

"Is he here?" Sasha asks.

I look over at Sasha again. I'm getting a bad feeling now.

"This is not the file you're looking for," Merc says, waving his hand like he's Obi-Wan Kenobi. But then his laugh stops and his smile fades. "This is something else. Something..." He looks over at Sasha. "Bigger. It's much bigger. There's two files, James. Ford and I got it open after Sasha gave it to him last year. And it's all money, brother. Accounts, man. Hundreds, maybe even thousands, of secret money accounts."

"Company money?"

Merc takes a long drag on his smoke and then blows out rings. "Yeah. Your precious Company has holdings everywhere, man."

"Where the hell did it come from?"

He looks at Sasha and I turn my head as well. She's got a grin on her face. But it's not one of satisfaction or amusement. It's nerves. "Spill, Smurf."

"My dad was drunk the night before that Christmas Eve job. I knew he had something important. He said he was going to California for a day the week before. He left me at home. Alone. He never does that. He takes me to my grandparents when he has out-of-town business. So I knew something was wrong that day. And when he came back, he had a flash drive."

"He didn't go to California," Merc says, interrupting the story. "Ford and I tracked him. He went to the Caymans and visited every bank in Georgetown."

"He was late," Sasha says sadly. "He didn't get back until the next day. I stayed home and worried the whole time."

"He set it up to steal all their money."

I laugh. "Define all."

"All. Except private funds, which I'm sure, from the lifestyle Nick describes, are still considerable."

"Fucking Nick. I'll kill that asshole for sending Harper away with the wrong file."

"I'm not sure Nick knows, James."

"So what's on *that* file? The file he gave Harper. I assumed it was just names and shit."

"Maybe it is," Merc says. "Or maybe it's not. But whatever it is, it's important to these people."

"None of this makes sense. Why the hell did the Admiral send me to the beach? Who the fuck is in charge of this operation?"

"I don't think it's one operation, James." Merc and I both look to Sasha. "I only hear and see snippets, so you have to understand that when I tell you this stuff. But I've seen and heard a lot. My dad used to be someone important. He was kicked out of that position and that's how we ended up on the road living out of an RV. But he still knew a lot of stuff. And right before he died, he was stealing their money and he was in contact with Nick. Nick had been around for months before the Christmas job. Nick is the one he was working with."

I just stare at her.

"Nick asked him for help in stealing all that money. My father did it, not Nick. But it was Nick's idea."

"Why the fuck didn't you two tell me this shit up front?"

Sasha steps back at my tone, but Merc has a hand on my shoulder before I can move.

"Look, dude, you were fucking insane, OK? We couldn't bring you in until we knew you'd snap out of it. And you did. So she brought you here."

"No." I shake my head. "I brought *her* here."

Merc smiles. "She's damn good, isn't she?"

"You set me up, Smurf?"

"Sorry," she says. But she's pretty proud of herself from the look on her face. "I was supposed to figure out if you were insane or not. Merc did send you to get me. But so did the Admiral. And Merc did send me out to the prairie to wait you out. But so did the Admiral. He's playing you, James. He told me to kill you and that's why he told you to kill me. And I'm pretty sure dropping Harper off was a bad idea, but we really did need to get rid of her."

I scrub my hand down my face as I process all this. "And you let me put Harper in danger… why?" I look up again and they both stop smiling. I know that look. I don't feel the change in me—I never feel the change in me. But I see the change in them.

"Now look, Tet," Merc says as he squeezes my shoulder tighter. "You were not supposed to see her."

"That's bullshit. The fucking Admiral sent me to the beach to watch her."

"He sent you to the beach so you'd bump into your assassin. But I paid that guy a visit before you arrived."

"More bullshit! I told you on the phone before I ever went to the beach that I failed my psych exam and you practically hung up on me."

"No, I said I didn't have time for your whining. And I didn't. I've got my own side jobs going, you know that. But the next day I took a trip down to SoCal and took care of your business."

"Was it One?" I ask

"Is One dead?" Merc quips back. I just give him a snide look. "Obviously it was not One." He waits to see if I'll take another guess but I don't. "It was Eight."

"So all those assassinate-the-assassin jobs I did over the past two years?"

He shrugs. "Setups, I guess. I really have no idea, Tet. They wanted them to appear dead, but not be dead. You tell me. You know these Company people. I don't. I have no clue how they think other than they want to get rid of me and I'm not gonna go easy."

"That makes no sense."

"Regime change, my friend," Merc says. "Someone else wants

to take over. Think about it. Harper poisons all those higher-ups when she makes her escape. You pick off your brother—for real," he adds. "Then you find Harper and trail her like a good dog. One barges in and steals her file in the last second. Why?"

"They don't trust me."

Merc laughs. "Would you trust you?"

"Whatever."

"I mean, I wouldn't trust you for shit." His smile says otherwise. "But I don't think that's the reason. I don't think they know about this file we have." He looks over to Sasha. "What do you think?"

She looks stunned that he wants her opinion. And why not ask her? She seems to be the one with all the answers, whether she wants to have them or not. Her expression becomes sad. Her eyes droop. "They know. They killed my dad for it."

"So why two files?" I look at Merc for this.

"From what I can tell, there's some kind of hack going on in the code. They need both files to access the money. And this makes sense. Because Ford and I tried like motherfuckers to steal money out of those accounts. I mean, shit. You dangle numbers in front of a hacker and that's just what we do. But fuck if we could figure it out."

"Nick would know."

Merc and I both look at Sasha at the same time.

"Nick will know what to do with it."

"Sasha," I say softly. "Look, you can't trust that guy. OK? You can't trust him. He put Harper in danger. He put you in danger. He's gotta be working for the Admiral."

SIX

Sasha

They shut up about Nick after that, so I take that as my cue to leave so they can share their secrets.

I understand what they're saying. Nick is part of this. Nick is setting us all up. Nick is not on our side. And I don't have the energy to defend him, because to be honest, I don't know him all that well. But they don't know him all that well either. Nick has been working other parts of the world his whole life. He's only in North America because he took off last year on his birthday. I don't think he's bad. I don't have any proof, I just don't think he is.

So I go out into the mall area and look around. It's near closing and there's hardly anyone around. I walk through my dad's corner booth—he has the largest one in the mall, it takes up the space of a dozen regular-sized booths—and my eyes rest on the other booth we run.

Mine.

He sold illegal guns to Company men and legal gear to the general public. But I sold girly stuff. Books. Jewelry. Knick-knacks. Dolls. I used to love dolls as much as I loved dinosaurs.

My fingers trace the glass-top cabinet as I walk into the little entrance of my booth and a layer of dust collects as I push it along. I used to man this booth myself and kept most of the stuff inside the cabinets. But I haven't been here since—

"Sasha?"

I turn towards the voice and put on one of my many fake expressions I've mastered over the past seven months. "Hi, Mrs. Sheldon. Long time no see." My plastic smile never wavers. I meet her tired old blue eyes as a girl who accepts that her life was torn apart and will never be the same.

"Oh, honey. I'm so happy to see you again. After the accident I never got a chance to say goodbye. And then the fire up at the ranch." She pulls me into one of those old-lady hugs where they squeeze you into their bosoms and starts to pet my hair.

She smells like rose water. Not a scent I care for, but it's very popular with the old ladies in this mall. I let her hug me because she doesn't know better. She doesn't know I'm a killer now. She doesn't know what I'm gonna do in the days ahead.

"How have you been, sweetie?"

I'm grateful for the opportunity to pull away and get the smell of her old satin coat lapels out of my nose. "I'm great. I live with my uncle now."

"Oh, he's such a blessing, taking over the store like that—"

"No, a different uncle," I interrupt her and force myself not to laugh. I have so many damn 'uncles' people just stopped asking. Now that Mrs. Sheldon has been reminded of that fact, she changes the subject.

"Where are you going to school now, dear? Still homeschool?"

"Yes, ma'am." When people ask about homeschool you gotta be extra special polite or else they think you're a serial killer in training. I almost snicker at that one. I should really stop calling myself a homeschooler. I soften the blow with a lie. "I'm going to private school this fall though, so I'll get the proper amount of government-mandated brainwashing before the cynicism sets in."

She smiles but her eyebrows are all slanted like Eric Cartman's when he's mad. I prepare myself for the next question, which would probably require me to give her an answer worthy of calling social services, but I'm ready for her to move on and leave me alone. So I say nothing. Just let the silence hang between us.

"Well," she says, finally taking the hint, "it was wonderful to see you again. You're so grown up now. You look like a proper young lady."

"Thank you," I say sweetly. And then I plaster that expression on my face and wait for her to leave.

She smiles for a few more seconds, then nods. "OK. I must run. Bye, dear."

"Byeeeee," I call out after her. She never looks back.

I walk over to Mrs. Sheldon's booth. She sells vintage clothing so she has a full-length mirror set up. I stand in front of it and take myself in. Harper is the only girl I know. We might not be friends, exactly. But I'm starting to think of her that way. So I compare myself to her.

I'm tall. I've definitely grown a couple inches this year. I'm not as tall as Harper, but I've only got an inch to go, I bet.

Blonde hair. It's longer now than it's ever been. James made me comb it in the truck, so it's almost tidy. Harper's hair is longer than mine. And more silky.

Blue eyes. They are not the striking kind of blue that some people have. Harper has brown eyes. They are light and mine are dark. A little bit muddy if you don't see them straight on.

Long legs. I have always had long legs. That's one thing I have over Harper, I think. She's got athletic legs. Like she works out. I don't work out.

Small breasts. These are new and I turn a little to get a better look at them, and then sigh. There's not much to see there. I should start wearing a bra though. I wonder if James will take me bra shopping?

I cackle to myself as I picture that. He's so easy to fuck with. How can a guy who's killed hundreds of people be so damn easy to fuck with?

I take one last look at myself and vow to buy some clothes that don't come from the Burlington ALCO if I live through this stupid plan.

And then I sigh and look back at my dad's booth. It feels like he could just come walking right out of the back room. That instead of Merc running this place for the last several months, it would be him.

"It's not, Sasha. So just get used to it. The only thing that matters now is revenge."

I can't believe I said that out loud.

I walk into the booth and start looking for clothes. I rummage around the vintage section until I find a pair of green army fatigues in a small enough size, and then I undress and pull them on real fast.

I find a white t-shirt and some old boots and put those on too.

And now… I feel like the *real* Sasha. It should make me smile, but instead it makes me nostalgic for the life I used to have. It might not have been anything special to people on the outside, but to me it definitely was.

I don't care about hunting or fishing. I could take or leave camping and survival training. But the thing is, I did all that stuff with my dad. He made all that stuff special.

And now that he's gone… well…I don't want to do it anymore. I don't want to ever set foot in the forest again. I don't want to shoot guns or bows. I don't want to camp or survive.

I just want to get even and then I want them all to leave me alone.

I turn my back on the store and walk back to my own booth. On the far table there's shards of wrapping paper and ribbon from the last day I was here. Christmas Eve. The day Merc came to buy guns and Ford came to buy presents. I allow a miniscule smile for Ford and then a small chuckle startles me as strong hands clasp over my eyes.

I react with an elbow to my attacker's ribs.

"Ow," he bellows. "I give! I give!"

His hands come down from my eyes and I whirl around with surprise and excitement. "Nick!"

He holds me by the shoulders and then pulls me in tight for a hug. "God, I was fucking worried about you."

"I'm fine," I say into his shirt as he holds me close. "Really," I say, pushing him back. I like Nick. And I think he likes me too, but not the way I like him. The fact that he's touching me makes me jittery in a way that freaks me out.

"Sasha." He holds my face in his hands and I have a moment

of panic that he will kiss me and then that changes to regret when he doesn't. "You look good, kid. A lot better than I imagined all these months."

I duck under his arm and scoot out of his grasp, making him turn. "You look good too. Far too good for a guy who's been on the run for a year."

He smirks at me and for a moment I think he's flirting. But then he pats his front pocket and pulls out a handful of suckers. Those little tiny ones they give away free in the old-lady booths here in the mall.

"You have got to be kidding me. You brought me candy? What am I, six?"

"Look," he says, fanning them out a little. "They're all butterscotch. Your favorite."

Aww. I might melt a little. He knows my favorite flavor. I take them, but he grabs one for himself and then bites off the wrapper and spits it out on the floor.

I just stare at his lips as he puts the sucker in his mouth and starts talking about how he stopped off at a truck stop on his way into town and picked through the canister until he found… oh, fuck. I have no idea what he's saying. I'm still looking at his mouth.

He's looking at me expectantly. "What?" I ask.

He pops that sucker out of his mouth and holds it out for me. "Here, I don't want it."

"Then why did you take it?" I ask, laughing. I take the sucker, not really sure what I'll do with it.

And then he leans into my space and slides his hands up into my hair. "I just wanted to lick it before you did."

A shotgun cocks off to the side of us and we both turn our heads slowly.

"You're gonna take your hands off my Smurf and back the fuck away."

Nick laughs but James does not look like he's joking. In fact, James looks like Tet right now. "Smurf?" Nick laughs again, only louder this time. "First of all, Six, if this Smurf belongs to anyone, it's me." He looks over at me. "Right, Sash?"

God, I'm so bad at choosing sides. So I hesitate. But that's OK, because James steps forward into Nick's space and looks down at him. James is an inch or so taller, so he can do that. "She's thirteen years old, Tate. If you touch her a minute before she's eighteen, I'll cut your fucking balls off."

Nick smacks the barrel of the shotgun away and huffs. "Don't be stupid. She's a kid." And then, as if that wasn't a kill shot through my heart, he says, "Which reminds me, I got a girl you might be interested in."

I stop listening. I just toss that butterscotch sucker into the trash and walk off. Merc stretches out an arm to clothesline me before I can pass him a few paces down, but I duck. He grabs again and gets a hold of my shirt. "Stay here, Sasha. You're not allowed to be alone anymore."

"What girl?" James asks.

Nick looks over at me and winks. I'm not sure what that means but James takes it as a signal that Nick and I are sharing secrets. But before I can deny it, Nick continues talking. "I'd love to tell you about it, but first, where the fuck is my sister?" He looks around, like she's gonna be here, hiding from him instead of squealing his name at first sight.

I don't think I've ever seen James speechless.

"Where the *fuck* is my sister?"

"I had to take her back to the yacht."

Nick doesn't even have words for that. He's stunned silent.

"One, man. I fucking..." James searches for words. But how to explain this clusterfuck? "He showed back up, drugged Harper. Gave her way too much..."

We stare at James in silence.

Then Nick attacks. It's a stupid move because James ducks, grabs his legs, and then body-slams him on the carpet in front of my booth. "Take easy, asshole. She's fine. I left her with the Admiral while I came looking for you."

"What the fuck is wrong with you?" Nick growls and flips James over. They both spring to their feet and circle each other. "Are you stupid?" he screams at James. "Do you have any idea what you just fucking did?"

No one answers and he doesn't tell us. He just turns and walks to the back room of my dad's booth.

SEVEN

Sasha

Merc's cabin has a strange bookshelf filled with vintage science fiction, hippy acid-tripping pop culture from the Seventies, and American classics. I have a sudden regret for leaving my *Little House* book back at the mall. It's a childish book. One more suited for ten-year-olds instead of me. But it has an innocence and simplicity about it that my life could use a little more of.

I pick a sci-fi novel off the shelf as a new song comes on my earbuds. Merc's idea. To shelter me from the manly conversation going on across the room. I take a quick glance over my shoulder and catch Nick in mid-swing. His fist crashes against Tet's jaw and then the whole thing starts all over again.

He's not taking this well. That's what Merc said when he gave me the iPod and earbuds. *Better stay out of it, kid.* And then he walked off.

Nick not taking this well is the understatement of the year. The fights have been numerous and loud. Short, but what they lack in length, they make up for in intensity. We still don't know why Nick is so pissed. At least, I never heard that explanation since we got here to this cabin just outside of town. Maybe Nick told Merc when they drove together? I rode with James and James didn't say shit on that drive.

Merc likes *Taking Back Sunday* and I like this song, so I hum along as I read the back cover of the sci-fi novel.

A thousand years after the apocalypse came to Earth and humans built a dome…

Yeah. No, thank you.

I put it back and sigh. The crashing of furniture makes me glance over my shoulder a second time, and now Merc is prying Nick and Tet apart.

Men. They are so emotional, it drives me crazy.

The next book is called *The Abortion.*

That one makes me laugh and then I have like an out-of-body vision of myself standing in this room looking through Merc's bookshelf, laughing at a book called *The Abortion*, while Tet and Nick try to kill each other.

There is no hope for this girl at all. Like zero chance of hope. I mean, it's just over. I put that book back and walk down the hallway to the bathroom. This cabin is weird. It's got three bedrooms and two bathrooms, but one bathroom is the laundry room too. And it has a door that leads out back.

Only a man would have a bathroom with a back door, but right now I'm glad it's here because I walk right out and into the late-afternoon sunshine. There's a picnic table down a rolling slope that leads into some woods, so I walk down and cop a squat on the table so I can prop my feet up on the seat and try and makes some sense of things.

One. That was certainly a surprise when he showed up in Huntington Beach. I'm not sure what Tet has in mind for him, and I'm not sure I even want to know. But whatever he does, I don't think I care too much.

I'm on James' side no matter what. I just can't see hitching my wagon to anyone else right now. He's the best at what he does. And we need the best. I'm sure Merc is a good killer too. And Nick. He's not dead yet, so he has to have a certain skill level.

But Tet. Now that man is a killer.

A shadow forms in front of me and I look up from my

introspection to see Nick walking down the hill. His mouth is moving so I know he's talking, but I can't hear anything because *Nothing At All* is blaring in my ears.

"What?" I say, removing my buds. I really like this song.

"Fucking James is out of his mind." He takes a seat next to me on the table.

"That's not James, Nick. That's Tet. And yeah. I agree."

"Why the fuck did he do it? Were you there?"

Shit.

I nod. "I was there. One drugged her and the Admiral wanted me dead. James had to produce a dead me and a live Harper. It was as simple as that."

He just stares at me like I'm a freak. "You're OK with this? That he gave my sister back?"

I hate his accusatory tone. And then his words from earlier pop into my mind. He has a girl. I'm just a kid. "I'm not OK with it, Nick. I just don't see much choice. We needed to buy time."

"So you sold my sister?" He scrubs his hands down his face. "Fuck. Sorry." He looks over at me and his blond hair falls into his eyes, obscuring his face a little. Making him look sad and dangerous and angry all at the same time. "But fuck, man. I was counting on that file and my sister, and now I got nothing, Sash." His eyes search mine. "Nothing. I'm right back where I started." He takes my hand and squeezes it. "Sorry. OK? For getting mad."

I nod. And I wish I could make him feel better by telling him about the other file, but I can't. I never did tell Nick. I never did tell anyone after Ford took the file to Merc. He said keep my mouth shut and I did. And now, even though Nick and I are on the same side… I'm not entirely sure that's true. Who is this girl he wants James to see? He's on the run. How does he have time to find girls?

So I don't say anything about the file. "James has a plan, I think."

"Yeah, to get us all killed."

I look away and Nick scoots closer to me on the table. "Sorry."

And then we sit in silence for a little while. Finally he tugs on the earbud draped over my shoulder closest to him. "What're you listening to?"

I look at the iPod in my hands and offer it up to Nick, but he puts a hand up and declines. "Is that why you came out here? To get away from me and James?" He reaches into his jeans pocket to pull out a smoke.

Sometimes I wish I could smoke. It looks relaxing. It's something all hunters do and I'm a hunter now. Plus, on the comparison scale, it's better than drinking. Most hunters don't do much of that. They are always alert. But Merc drinks a lot. I like that about him. "Nah," I say as he lights up his cigarette. "I just wanted to be alone."

Nick smiles at me and a small flutter forms in my stomach against my better judgment. I'm not immune to his charm. And he *is* charming. Harper is very beautiful in a striking model kind of way. Nick is her twin, and his beauty is more surfer than model, but nonetheless, it's a bit overwhelming. So a stomach flutter is in order. "I missed you, ya know."

I give him a smirk and a head tilt to show him I'm playing. "I would've never known by the way you disappeared. How come you left me?"

"Hey," he says, putting his hands up like he's surrendering. "I told you we had to lie low. I was in hiding."

"That makes no sense, Nick. Harper was under surveillance, so the Admiral always knew where she was. How come he didn't just come take her?"

"He was waiting for the file. Believe me, they looked for that fucker all year and couldn't find it. I suppose that's why they sent Tet in. And look what happened? That fucker got it."

"One got it."

"Yeah, but Tet would've had it if One hadn't taken it. Harper walked right into his trap."

"You don't like James, do you?"

"It's got nothing to do with liking him, Sash. It's got everything to do with trusting him. And now we gotta go back and get that fucking file. And Harper. And don't you think they know I'm coming now? I mean fuck, our birthday is only a few days away."

"What's that got to do with it?" My mind is spinning. There is so much going on.

"Never mind," he says as he tries to lace our fingers together, but I pull my hand away before he can take it. "What the fuck?"

"It's not worth it," I say.

"What's not worth it?"

I nod my head in the direction of the cabin up the hill. "The fight you'll have with Tet if you hold my hand."

Nick's eyes shoot up to the top of the hill where Tet is standing with his arms crossed. "Fucking freak," Nick says, blowing out a long puff of smoke.

"Hey," I say, nodding at his cigarette. "Can I bum one of those?"

His eyes dart back to Tet, just a fraction of a second. But I see it. "You're too young to smoke, kid."

That's all I needed to know. "I was just messing with you." I reach over and ruffle up his hair and he automatically dodges. I smile at him and he shoots me an uneasy one back. "Well, I'm going back in and see if Merc will teach me how to play *Kumbaya* on the guitar. Wanna come?"

He glances up at Tet again and shakes his head. "When I'm done here."

"OK." I hop down and swat the dirt off my butt as I walk back to the top of the hill. Tet turns and walks with me as we head back to the cabin together.

"You hungry, Smurf?" James asks.

"Starved."

"Me too." And then he opens the back door and lets me walk through.

Like I said. James is a dream in the partner department.

It's Tet you gotta worry about.

EIGHT

Sasha

We go back inside and Merc is sitting at the kitchen table smoking. That seems to be the thing to do when shit goes down. And now I really do want to learn to smoke but I have to settle for pulling out a butterscotch sucker from my pocket.

The screen door in back slams and Nick follows us in.

"Sasha," he says. I turn reluctantly. I know that tone and it says I'm about to be in the middle of something.

"What?"

"Get your shit. We're leaving."

"She's not leaving with you," Tet says. He grabs my hand in case I make a break for it.

"Why, Tet? So you can keep using her the way you did Harper? So you can drag her into your insane revenge scheme? This shit is between you and One, man. Or you and my father. But I'm gonna say this one time. We're leaving. I'm gonna go finish the job you didn't, and then you're gonna stay the fuck out of my life. You stay away from my sister and you stay away from my promise." Nick points his finger at me and then his gaze follows. "Go get your stuff." And then he pulls out a gun and points it at James. "Try and stop her."

"Nick," I say.

"I'm not gonna say it again, Sash. Now get what you need."

I look over at James but he's got nothing to say to me. Not even a nod. So I do what I'm told. I got to the last bedroom, grab the pack I set on the floor earlier, and shrug it onto my back as I walk back out to the living room.

"I'm going back to get her, Nick," James is saying as I enter the room. He's sitting down at the table next to Merc now, like those two haven't a care in the world. Like Nick isn't standing here in the living room with a gun. And I'm sure if they really wanted to fuck Nick up, he and Merc could do it. But Nick, no matter what he does, is part of the plan.

"Look, asshole. You have no idea what you're doing."

James nods with a smirk. "Right. I didn't get this far by not understanding the game."

"Dude, they're using you. And every time I hear about it, I think to myself, 'Nah, Six is so much smarter than that.' And then every time you fall for it. But this time, asshole—this time I'm all out of faith. I asked you to do one thing for me. Keep her out of it. And what do you do? You deliver her to the one person who will bring her into it."

"Bring her into it how?" Merc asks. "I mean, look, Nick, I'm the first to admit I have no clue what you people are doing. But we've been on the same side all year. So it's better to work through the team problems than split up."

Nick points to me but he's looking at Merc. "She's not on the team, Merc. Yet here she is, fully planning on participating. And you know why?" He looks at James now. "Because this asshole wants to use her. Just like he uses all the people he drags into his schemes. And now Harper's in it. Didn't your father ever teach you anything, Tet? Women and children stay home."

"Yeah, so they can be sold. They're commodities."

Nick actually nods at that. "Yeah, maybe that's how I see them then. Investments. The future. So shoot me."

"We'll meet you at the yacht," James says casually.

"She's not on the yacht, you fuck. How many ways do I have

to say it? You sent her back to the one person she should never see again. She's as good as gone now. If I don't get to her by next week, she's as good as gone."

"So," Merc says. "Let's go get her now. It's only been a couple days."

Nick's eyes burn but his words are eerily calm now. "It's too late. He gave her away by now."

"What?" James says, getting to his feet. "What the fuck are you talking about?"

"Last year, on our eighteenth birthday? That wasn't the one."

"The one what?" Merc says, throwing his hands up. "Will you stop talking in fucking code? Just spit it out."

Nick looks at James for a long second. "He's been using you, man. She's been promised since she was six, all right. But it was never to you. And in a few days, when we turn nineteen, my father's gonna make good on that promise."

"Where?" James seethes.

"The Santa Barbara house. There's gonna be a big party. Her promise, James. I gotta tell you—"

And for a second I really think he will. I really think that Nick is gonna tell James the one thing he needs to know that he has no idea he needs to know. James feels it too. A shift in what's happening here. A shift from potential to realized consequences.

James takes a step forward but there's a snapping sound and then he's gone. Dropped down. Or hit. Bullets spray into the house. I scream and duck, but then someone has my hand and I'm dragged to the back of the house.

NINE

Sasha

"Sasha, run!" Nick is pulling me out the back door and we run so fast down the hill, I fall face first and roll. Nick scoops me up and carries me a few paces, then sets me down and runs again. No yelling this time, at least not for us. But behind us the gunfire is still rattling off. AK's spitting out bullets.

After a few minutes the gunfire stops. Nick pulls me down a ridge dotted with pine trees and then we both slip because the incline is so severe and we are a human landslide. Rocks and clumps of dirt splatter out in front of our boots and then we plop to the ground and keep running. There's no trees here and Nick runs faster. "Hurry, Sash. Hurry," he prods me.

But my stitch in my side is so painful, my pathetic attempts to suck in air so painful... "I can't, Nick. I can't run anymore."

He ignores that, just pulls me along until we get under the cover of the pines. "Just a little farther," he huffs as he boosts me up the side of a small cliff by the butt. He climbs up after me and takes my hand again. "Hurry, hurry, hurry. We need to get out of here before they come looking."

"Who?" Jesus. My heart is beating so fast I think I might die. My phone buzzes in my pocket.

"Answer it," Nick barks at me. And then he stops, tugging me to stop with him when momentum takes me forward. "Give me your phone."

I jerk my hand from his and shake my head. "No. Tell me what's going on."

"Who's calling you?"

"How the hell should I know?"

"Look," he growls in my face. "Look who it is."

I take my phone out and Nick snatches it away and presses the answer tab. "Merc. Yeah," he barks into the phone. I can just barely make out words on the other end. Nick's eyes shift around for a few seconds, then rest back on mine. "Got it." And then he ends the call and hands it back. He starts walking over to a hill covered in dead pine needles.

"Well?" I ask.

"James is dead."

My heart stops. "He is *not.*"

"He's missing and they threw grenades inside the cabin. He's dead."

"No," I say firmly. "No. He can't die."

Nick is looking for something on the little slope. He lets out a grunt and then pulls. The whole hill slides away and I think I'm hallucinating before I realize it's a cover that has pine needles stuck to it to make it look like brush-covered ground. There's a motorcycle underneath.

"You planned this?"

He shoots me a look. "I plan for everything. Except your boyfriend back here giving my sister away."

"Boyfriend?"

"James is awfully attached to you, Sash. And as far as I can see"—Nick swings his leg over the bike and turns the ignition to start the engine—"there's only two possibilities for that. He likes you, which would be weird, because he says he loves Harper, yet he sold her out to my dad. Or he needs you for something." Nick stares me in the eyes. "I'm pretty sure he's using you. Grab the helmets and get on the bike. We're leaving."

I hand him a helmet from the ground and then plop the other one on my head. "Where are we going?" I ask, swinging my leg over.

"To set things right, Sash. Whatever it takes, I'm gonna set things right."

"What about Merc?"

"He says he's out."

What?

Nick gives the throttle some gas and we spring forward. This bike is not off-road capable, but we're only on the dirt for about a mile when a paved road appears. He doesn't stop to tell me where we're going, he just takes that road all the way to the interstate and before I know it, we're heading west.

And all I do for the next four hours is think about how my life just changed again.

James is gone.

TEN

Sasha

"Sash," Nick whispers in my ear.

I brush him away and roll over, still very sleepy after yesterday. We stopped in Rock Springs to grab dinner since towns are few and far between out here, and by the time we were done, Nick wanted to get a room for the night.

"Sash," he repeats. "Wake up. Let's go eat and hit the road."

"What time is it?"

"A little after seven."

I groan. "Are we in a hurry?" Silence. I open one eye and look at him. He's lying next to me, one cheek pressed against the same pillow. His brown eyes are scrunched up like he's confused. "What?"

"I'm sorry for those things I said yesterday. I wasn't thinking clearly."

I just stare at him.

"He might not be dead."

I can't say anything, because if I do, I'll cry.

"He's not dead. He's Tet, for fuck's sake. OK? He's not dead."

But we called Merc last night after we got the room and Merc said he can't find him. "I think he's dead," I finally say.

Nick lets out a long breath. "We won't know until we know, Sash. But… even if he is, he'd want me to keep going. He'd want Harper to be safe. And now that I know she's back with my father, she's not safe, Sash. I have to go get her. And get that fucking file."

I roll over on the bed and turn my back to him. "You shouldn't have let Harper have it if it's so valuable."

"She was safer with it, Sasha. It gave her power."

"It almost got her killed." I turn back over. "She was dead. James saved her." I look away. "He saved me too," I mumble.

"What's the deal with the two of you?"

I sit up and throw the covers off because obviously sleep time is over. "What do you mean?" I'm still fully clothed so I just slip my feet into my boots and straighten my ponytail.

Nick gets up off the bed and when I turn to look at him, his scowl is even more pronounced. "He was possessive of you. He threatened me. Why was he acting that way? How long have you really known him?"

It's my turn to squint my eyes. "A week? You know that, Nick. We talked about it before he came to get me. And a lot of good it did, making me stay out there for three fucking months."

"Watch your mouth," Nick snaps.

I flip him off and shoot him a look. "Don't boss me around. I'm in a very bad mood."

"I told you why you had to stay out there. The Admiral sent you to wait for Tet and when the Admiral gives you an order, you follow it."

"Yeah, but you knew when James was coming. You knew he was in the OC with Harper. So explain why we didn't just get a hotel in the next town over and wait him out there."

Nick walks towards me smiling. I step back. But he grabs my arm and pulls me close. "We could've done that, Sasha." He looks down on my face. I hate the fact that he's so much bigger than me. I hate the fact that everyone is so much bigger than me. "But I like you, ya know. I like you and I don't think I'd have been very good at keeping my hands to myself if we were bunking together for months." He laughs. "I mean, I know you're too young in my head, but you know, I'm just a eighteen-year-old guy."

My cheeks heat up and I'm not sure if I'm blushing because he said that to me, or if I'm creeped out that he's thinking about me sexually. "That's bullshit," I finally say. "You know you're not allowed to touch me until I'm eighteen. I don't think you have a self-control problem. I think you're just up to other things and you don't want me to know about them."

"We're not operating inside the Company boundaries, Sash. We can make our own rules if we want. And yeah to the last part too. I'm up to a whole bunch of shit that you will never know about. That's life. You're a girl. I'm a guy. You should be in school right now."

"School?" I don't even have a comeback for that. "What the hell world are you living in? I'm a Company kid with a hit on my head. What fucking school am I supposed to be in?"

"Language," he whispers as he places his fingertips against my lips.

My whole body shudders. But I shrug it off and blink at him. "I'd love nothing more than to go back to school and grow up like a normal kid. But if I do that, then we're not promised anymore."

He tisks his tongue and tightens his grip around me as I wriggle to break free. "Is that what you want?"

"I have no idea what I want. But why I don't want is you telling me what to think or how to act. Or just assuming I'm going along with your plans every second of the day. I'm one half of this team so I expect to be treated like a partner."

He leans down until his warm breath skates across my ear. "We are partners, Sash. In every sense of the word. You were given to me, so you're mine. But I'm not putting up this big resistance as a pretense, you understand. I'm doing this to change the future for all the Company kids who come after us. So if you think I'm bound to that promise your father gave under duress when you were born, you're wrong. I don't need a promise to get a wife. I'm quite capable of getting married all on my own. So"—his hand slides around the back of my neck and his fingertips slip up into my hair, sending chills down my whole body—"let's just forget that promise right now and be together because we like each other."

He smiles as I stare dumbly up at him and then he laughs and lets go of my head. His fingers slip through my hair, dragging against the sensitive skin of my scalp. And then they are gone. "Sasha Cherlin, I have something cool to tell you. Do you want to hear it?"

I swallow. "Is it something good?"

He nods and smiles. "Yeah. Come sit." He walks over to the edge of the bed and sits down, then pats the mattress for me to follow.

I sit, but not too close. I don't really know what's happening.

"I was bumming around up in the mountains in Wyoming. Way the fuck out by Bighorn Lake. You know it, right?"

I shoot him a look. "Everyone knows where Bighorn Lake is."

He laughs. "So I was up there in the mountains and I was so fucking lost. But there was like this park access road, so I walked up this road to the top of a hill and do you know what was up there?"

I shake my head as I stare into his eyes. He's excited to tell me this and that makes me excited with him. "What was it?"

"That medicine wheel thing you were talking about last summer. Remember that?"

My throat starts to sting and my eyes start to water. "I was just talking to James about that a few days ago."

"Huh," Nick says, smiling. "I saw it." He looks over at me and then his hand grips my shoulder and he flops backwards on the bed, taking me with him. We sigh together. "It was pretty cool. You're gonna love seeing it."

"I'm not going," I say quickly. "I don't want to go." He says nothing to that. Just lets the silence take over until I feel the need to explain. "My dad was gonna take me this summer. I don't want to see it with anyone else."

"Hmmm. I can see your point. I mean, your dad would probably be mad if you went without him, don't you think?"

I tisk my tongue. "Just don't."

"What? That's your reason, right?"

I stare up at the ceiling.

"Because I know your dad was like that. All pissy about you being happy without him."

"I know it makes no sense to you, but it does to me. There's just no one else I want to see it with."

Nick turns his head to the side. "Sasha," he says. I turn mine too, and our faces are but a few inches apart. "I love you."

I feel the tears well up.

"I love you and I only want what's best for you. I want you to go to school. And live in a house. And never pick up a gun again. I want you to wear dresses and go to dances. And have dates with boys who take you to eat hamburgers. I want you to study dinosaurs and travel the world looking for clues about the past that no one else cares about."

He stops and swallows. Like he needs to build his courage up. Another tear streaks across my face until his fingertips intercepts it just as it rounds my nose.

"And once you've done all that without me, you're gonna realize that you can love more than once in a lifetime."

"You're going to be there with me," I blurt as the tears pour out. "You're my promise."

He shakes his head. "The promise is over. You have to forget about it. You have to move forward and forget about it. And if your dad was here, he'd tell you to go see that medicine wheel."

"We can go together, Nick. We can go up there together and you can show it to me."

But he's shaking his head before I'm even done. "I'm not going back."

"I'm not going back either."

He huffs out a small breath of air. I'm not sure if it's a laugh or a sign of resignation. "Are you hungry?"

I nod.

"What do you want?" He stares at me. Stares *into* me.

"Pancakes," I whisper.

"Then pancakes you shall have. I'll go get them and you take a shower."

And then he gets up and walks to the table to pick up his keys. "Get up," he calls as he walks to the door. "I'll be right back with the food."

I get in the shower and let the hot water blast down on me. I'm just rinsing off the conditioner in my hair when I hear the room door open and close. I finish rinsing and then step out of the shower, wrapping the towel around me tightly. The room door opens and closes again and I peek my head out of the bathroom. "Nick?"

There's no one in the room.

"Nick?"

I walk out and spot the food on the table. It's wrapped up tightly in a plastic bag to keep it warm. But it's what's next to the food that stops my heart.

Money.

I walk over and pick it up, counting in my head. Four hundred dollars. There's a folded piece of paper underneath the money and even though I do not want to pick that paper up and read what he wrote, I know I have to.

My hands tremble as I read his words.

Dear Sash,

I'm so sorry. But you and Harper—you two are the only reason I'm doing this. And if I took you with me, I'd be just as bad as my father. I'd be just as bad as James. I'm coming back, don't worry. I paid the room up for two weeks and I'll be back. I'll find you a home, Sasha. I swear. You're gonna have that life I told you about. Just stay here. Don't call anyone. Don't leave. Just please, stay here so I know you're safe.

I can't be your promise, it's wrong. But you're the only girl I've ever wanted. I hope you know that.

Nick

I cry silent tears as I read it over and over again. I never get dressed, just fall back on the bed in my towel as I try and come to terms with what's happening to my life.

I am thirteen years old.

I'm homeless.

My family is dead.

James might be dead.

Harper is in big trouble.

My promise walked out on me.

Can it get any worse?

I have no idea how long I lie there before I get up and fish my phone out of my pocket and call Merc.

"Yeah," he says after picking up on the first ring.

"I need you to come get me."

"I'm on my way to Jackson. I'm out, man. You and Nick are gonna have to figure this shit out yourselves. I know when to cut my losses."

"Nick left me in a hotel in Rock Springs. He's going to save Harper himself and get that file back. How can you be out? You have the other half of the file."

He's silent for a few moments and then he lets off a long sigh. "If I come get you, we're heading to my place in Jackson."

"No," I say firmly. "We're heading to Santa Barbara where Nick thinks they took Harper. You owe me, Merc. You owe me. And this is what I want. I want to go to Santa Barbara and help Nick."

"Kid, we're gonna need an army to help Nick now. They are dead serious about killing us and going to meet them on their own territory is one of the more stupid ideas Nick has had lately."

"I don't care. I'm in, Merc. I have very few good things to hold on to in my life. James, Harper, and Nick are pretty much all I have left. And I'm not gonna let him go fix this shit alone. OK? So come get me.

Nothing but silence on the other end. But then Merc grumbles. "Fuck. I'm like two hours away. Where the hell are you?"

I tell him the name of the hotel and then I hang up and get dressed. I eat the pancakes because they came from Nick, but I have to force them down. And then I stuff the money in my pocket along with the room key and sit in front of the window until Merc's truck pulls up in the parking lot.

I walk out the door and climb in the passenger side.

Merc takes out a smoke and lights it up, blowing smoke rings out the window as we head back out on the highway. "Do you know where the Santa Barbara place is? Because I sure don't."

I sigh. "I shouldn't know. But I do."

He laughs. "That's the story of your life, kid."

Ain't that the truth? "We need an army, you said?" I look up at him, but he's staring straight ahead. "I know where we can get an army."

"I bet you do."

And then he slides his shades down his face and turns up the music.

PART TWO

ELEVEN

Harper

The rolling of the ship eases me out of my slumber.

I'm home.

That thought bounces around my head for several seconds before I remember this is not home. I'm on my father's yacht. I don't open my eyes and I don't stop breathing heavily. Instead, I give off a long sleepy sigh and turn over. I crack one eye to figure out if I'm alone in the room.

"How are you feeling?" my father asks.

Not alone.

"It's wearing off, Harper. The doctor gave you a drug to make it wear off. I hope you realize we only drugged you so that Tet would leave quietly. But you became combative the last few times we brought you out of it—"

The last *few* times?

"—and since you've been known to make rash and dangerous decisions, we were forced to subdue you."

Well. Since there's no use pretending I'm still asleep, I open both my eyes. He's staring down at me and he looks worried, but then he smiles.

I hate to admit that it's reassuring. He's my father. It's hard to turn that off.

"How are you feeling?" he asks again. "OK?" His smile makes the corners of his eyes crinkle up. My father is handsome, even at fifty-one. His hair is not gray, it's still dark and it's still thick. His suit, however, is gray. And his tie is navy blue. When I was a girl I always loved to touch them. "Harper, answer me."

I pause for a few seconds and then nod. "I'm OK."

His smile grows and I get a warm feeling that I don't immediately understand. I mean, who is this man? How can he call himself my father when he's part of this organization and all they want is to marry me off?

"We're having dinner in an hour. I've had them prepare your favorites to welcome you home."

I don't know what to say to that, so I look away.

"Harper," he says sternly so I refocus on him. "I'm glad you're home."

I don't know what to say to that either.

"Did you even miss me?"

Why is he asking me these things?

"Because this ship was not the same without you two."

I look up at him for that. "Is Nick here?"

"No."

I look away.

"He's hiding. But once he hears you're back, he'll come for you, Harper. I know he will."

"So I'm a trap to catch him?"

"Why in the world do you think I'm trying to catch him? He's a grown man now. He can do as he pleases. I admit, he's messed up my plans for you two. But I'm not wholly dissatisfied about that."

I glance at him again. "You're not?"

"Why would I be unhappy that you were not given away on your birthday, Harper? I love you. I might not have been the perfect father, but I was present more than most parents in this modern world. I did my business on the ship to stay near you. I really do not understand where this distrust comes from."

"You promised me to someone."

"I had to. It's required. Which is why I'm not upset that didn't happen."

"James said you promised me to him."

"Tet is mistaken."

"I remember him, though. From the beach party when we turned Six."

"He said no, Harper. I gave him the opportunity and he said no. That was the end of it for me."

"But you sent for him every year."

This makes him hesitate. "Tet told you that?"

"James told me that."

My father sucks in a breath through clenched teeth. "It would be a very big mistake to mix them up, Harper. James is not Tet, and Tet is not James."

I get a really sick feeling in my stomach at that comment. "What are you talking about?"

"He's insane. He's been this way for a very long time. Years."

"Then why is he still working?"

My father smiles like he feels sorry for me. "Let's catch up over dinner. OK? Can you sit up?"

"I'm sure I can."

"I'd like you to sit up so I can make sure you're not dizzy."

I huff out a long sigh and then wiggle around until I prop myself up. I am dizzy, so I close my eyes and his steadying hand is on my shoulder. "I'm OK," I say. But there's something poking me in the butt, so I reach around and pull out my cell phone.

I look up at my father and wait for him to take it away.

He shrugs. "You're a grown woman, you're not a prisoner here, Harper. If that's your phone, you are welcome to use it." He lets that sink in for a few seconds, and then he nods and walks towards the cabin door. "One hour, Harp. Clean up and dress nicely, please."

And then he and the doctor walk out, closing the door behind them.

I sigh again and look around. It's my same room. This is my favorite yacht. The sailing ship.

Why is he being so nice? Not that my father was ever abusive towards me, but I poisoned thirteen people when I left. I ran away with no explanation.

It's true he never paid much attention. He was certainly never this doting. But this whole act right now seems to be one of… *concern.*

Is it real? Is it possible that Nick led me to believe we were in danger from him for reasons that were unfounded?

Do I need to start questioning my trust in my twin?

I don't have the energy for it. The drugs might be wearing off, but my head isn't working right. I feel a little sick. And the slight rolling motion of the yacht is not helping.

I look down at the phone and press the little button to wake it up. There's a message from James.

I look around nervously. I can't believe my father would just let me receive messages like this. I mean, I don't get it. He said I'm not a prisoner, but you don't drug someone and force them to come aboard your ship if they're not being kidnapped.

But then again he's my father and this is… was… might still be… my home. Is it really kidnapping?

I open the message and read it.

I'm sorry.

I bet he is. Asshole. I want to talk to him, but not yet. I need to have dinner to clear my head and think straight. I need to get a grip on what's happening.

I swing my legs over the side of the bunk and stand up, stumbling my way to the head attached to my cabin. I'm not used to being on a ship anymore and it both frightens and thrills me that I've lost my sea legs. Frightens me because that was my whole life before I left. The sea. The ship. The sailing. I don't want to lose that part of me. It's who I am.

But I'm excited about having been away for so long. Living at the beach. Seeing the world from the opposite perspective. Living on my own.

That makes me smile. And yes, I was quite the mess for most of that. But I did it.

I'm excited that I met James and had sex. Jesus. If my dad found out about that, I'm not sure what he'd do. I don't think James was sent to fuck me.

I really want to talk to him and it's killing me to wait. But I need to play this right. I feel like I'm part of a game. I'm a chess piece. I'm a card that's being held or played. I'm not quite sure.

But I do know one thing. Actions have consequences. I can't afford to mess this up.

So dinner it is. It's late, I know that. Because when I look out my porthole, I see nothing but black. The ship is rocking some, but it doesn't feel like we're moving, so we must still be in port.

OK. So I need to dress and go above deck for dinner.

I walk to my locker and open it. I recognize a few things. A bathing suit. Some flipflops. A beach bag. But other than that, the dresses are all new. I have six. One for each night of the week. This is how it's always been. One dress for each day I'm expected for dinner. We never had dinner on Sundays so I never needed seven dresses. And that kinda set the standard for how many sets of clothing I required. I have six pairs of shorts folded neatly on a shelf. And six tank tops on the shelf above. I have two pairs of shoes besides the flip flops. One fancy, one casual.

James asked me if I was spoiled and I said yes. But that's only because of how I was brought up. Not what I was given. I've never had an abundance of things. There's just not enough room on a ship, even one this size, for collections.

We went shopping six times a year. Every two months. And on each trip a new wardrobe was purchased for me. Six of this, six of that. Six, six, six. My life has always been about sixes.

How strange.

I mean, there's seven days in a week. Why not seven outfits?

I push the hangers aside so I can take a look at each option, and then choose a light yellow sun dress that has a beige knitted cropped sweater that barely covers my shoulders.

I slip on the fancy sandals. No heel. *That's only practical for a young lady on a boat*, the nanny had explained why I couldn't have stilettos as footwear. And then I look at myself in the mirror on the inside of the locker.

I have no idea who this girl is.

She's not Harper Tate who left here last year. That girl never ran away and changed her name. Or had her own apartment in Huntington Beach. Or had a beautiful man face-fuck her in a hallway.

That girl was a virgin and this girl is not.

God, I miss James. An overpowering, stabbing pain weighs down on my chest. Not a physical pain. But one that twines with my mind and can only be described as… heartbreak.

Did James betray me or not?

Did he leave me here to fend for myself? Or will he come back like he promised?

That's the only thing I can hold on to at the moment. He told me that before he left so I'd remember it.

He's coming for me.

I just need to be patient.

But I don't even know how long I was out. From the rumbling in my stomach and the need to pee, it must've been a long time.

The phone is resting on the bunk where I left it. I want to text him or call him so badly.

Just be patient, Harper. See what your father is up to. Because something is off here. Something is off and I need to know what that is before I make any decisions.

I take a deep breath and close the locker door. OK, it's just dinner. It's my father, for Pete's sake. I've had dinner with my father for as long as I can remember.

In fact, this is all starting to feel very familiar.

Almost comfortable.

Like I didn't kill thirteen people with poison a year ago, then steal the boat's tender and take a plane to LA to start a new life.

It feels… like that never happened.

It feels… like I've been forgiven.

Or maybe… it feels like a mission accomplished and a well-deserved homecoming.

I walk calmly down the hall and climb the ladder that will take me up to the main level, then turn the corner and climb again until I can feel the cool sea breeze of a summer night.

Yes. This *is* my home. The sea triggers all those familiar feelings of safety and comfort.

I can hear my father talking to the staff in the above-deck dining room and he sounds relaxed and at ease. But why shouldn't he be? He's the one in total control here. I glance out at the Orange County city lights. The harbor is a busy place, so there is a lot to look at. I wish I was out there. As much as I do like this ship, I didn't come here of my own free will. So regardless of what my father says, I *am* a prisoner.

The above-deck dining area is really built for partying. In fact, that's what it's called on the ship map hanging in the casual dining area a deck below. The party deck.

The area is open on three sides, with half walls that give the appearance of a room and a ceiling, with subtle, atmospheric lighting. The living area seats fifteen. There's a fireplace, two couches, an assortment of chairs, a coffee table, and a bar off to the side. The furniture is comfortable and stylish, but it's made to withstand the elements. The salty sea and the blazing sun.

On the other side of the living room is the dining table. The head and foot of the table do not have chairs. They have small couches similar to a settee. My father is sitting in the one on the port side, while my place is the same exact spot on the starboard side of the table.

"Ah," my father says as he stands, placing his napkin on the table as he waves me over to the other place. "You look better. How are you feeling, Harper?"

"Fine." I don't mean to answer him so quickly. I actually think it's a bad idea to talk to him at all until I get more of my bearings. But old habits die hard.

When my father asks you a question, you respond politely. And that's exactly what I did.

I walk over to the place set for me and wait for the staff to pull my chair out and then push me in.

I don't recognize my attendant and my father must notice that I'm wondering who he is, because he says, "Davis is… no longer with us."

"Oh." Does that mean he quit? Or does that mean I killed him with the others when I poisoned the water last summer?

I don't ask and he doesn't offer. But I know it's the latter.

I have to swallow hard to get past that realization. Davis was a part of my life since I was born. I'm a terrible person. A terrible, evil person.

I push that thought away and pick up my napkin, placing it on my lap like the lady I am. I have impeccable manners in a formal setting.

The servers appear with bottled water and they place one down in front of me.

I look at my father and he smiles. "You can't be too careful."

I just stare at him.

"Did you make a call to your James, then?"

I shake my head. "No, sir."

"Why not?" my father asks, as he holds his empty glass out for the staff to take and then accepts a new drink. He prefers whiskey. Good, strong, American whiskey. Which is funny, if you ask me. Because it's so cheap. You'd think a man with all his money would move on to Scotch or brandy. Isn't that what refined men on boats drink in books?

"I have nothing to say to him," I whisper.

The server brings me a salad. The greens are the kind that taste sweet and not bitter. My father gets the bitter leaves. So he really did have this meal made specially for me. Why?

I lift my salad fork and start to eat.

"Harper?" my father asks as soon as I take a bite, forcing me to grab my napkin and swallow down the food in a rush so I can answer.

"Yes?"

"Did he touch you?"

"Who?" I ask, stunned at his gall and pissed off at his intrusion.

"Tet."

"Of course he touched me."

My father stares hard at me. Probably not sure what I meant by that. But I don't give a shit. If he wants to know if I fucked James, let him come out and ask me. I take another bite of salad as I wait for his reaction.

He surprises me by looking down at his food and dropping the subject.

Score one for Harper. Because I did not lie. And bonus points for making the great Admiral squirm, even if it was just internally.

"So tell me about your days."

"My days?" I repeat, like I'm confused. But I'm not confused. At least not about his question. I'm confused as to what the hell he's actually doing here. "Most of them were pretty boring. I stayed inside a lot."

"That's not what I heard. I was told you left every morning and evening to exercise on the beach."

"Did James tell you that?"

"No, Number One told me that."

I drop my fork. "You mean the guy who drugged me?"

"Yes, well. He wasn't always so insubordinate. He was my best assassin until Tet took him out."

"But obviously James did not take him out."

"Obviously, James didn't do anything. I told you, do not mix them up." My father chews and then swallows. "Tet is a mess."

"Hmm."

My father smiles an indulgent smile, like such matters are above my level of comprehension. "Let me guess. Tet gave you that old spiel about mothers being killed and fathers standing by."

I just stare at my plate as I shuffle the green leaves around.

"He's insane, Harper. Long gone. He's killed hundreds of people for the Company. And actually," my father says, then stops to wipe his mouth and motion for the servers to remove his salad, "that number is so high, it might be in the thousands."

"I don't believe you," I whisper.

"I'm sure. It's improbable that one mad man could cause so much death and destruction. But he has. He's the best we've ever had. And do you know why, Harper?" My father doesn't wait for my answer. "Because he's been conditioned since he was very small to not care about people. He's been conditioned to lie and cheat. He's been conditioned to get whatever he needs, any way he can. And he's still alive today because he learned that lesson better than anyone else. Do you think I haven't tried?"

"Tried what?" I just stare at my father, not sure if he just admitted to trying to kill James or reform him.

"But right now he's being a good dog. Fetching that file for me. He's got a vendetta with One. One has it. I want it. Tet is the perfect man for that job. And," my father adds with a sly smirk, "it's forced him to keep his deal with me. To deliver you."

"You're lying."

"I'm not. He agreed to find you and bring you back after you showed him the file. But One..." My father shakes his head. And then he belts out a laugh unexpectedly. A guffaw that echoes off the ceiling. "Do you want to know the really funny part?"

I'm thinking no, but my father certainly isn't paying any attention to what I want.

"The really funny part is that I sent every assassin I had off to kill Tet over the past few years."

He stares at me, smiling, as I think about this for a few moments. "It didn't work," I say, my words just as unexpected as his laugh. "He told me… he told me he killed them all."

"All but one."

"Number One?"

"No, Harper. He *thought* he killed One, but One has other plans. So even though One tricked him, that was still a score in Tet's mind. No, the job he never finished was Number *Zero*."

"I don't know all their numbers," I say, like we're talking about current affairs or the weather, and not men who kill people on command.

"Of course not. But you've met her. Watched him finish her off just a couple hours ago."

My stomach rumbles and I just stare at my father, horrified.

Sasha.

How could I have forgotten that James shot Sasha?

And just as I'm thinking that the boat begins to move. "Are we leaving?"

"Did you really forget?" my father asks me, ignoring my question.

My breathing is speeding up and I have the familiar heart palpitations. The sweat starts to gather on my brow and I have to close my eyes and breathe deeply to stop the chain reaction.

A strong hand touches me on the shoulder. "I'm sorry. I thought you were playing a game. I didn't realize you hadn't remembered. She was your friend?"

He hands me the bottle of water and I twist the cap until the plastic seal breaks and I take a sip.

"I don't know why Tet didn't kill her as he was instructed. I don't understand why the child didn't finish the job I sent her to do. She had the element of surprise and she handled herself very well when I sent the assassins to kill her grandparents. So the only thing I can assume is that they were playing off each other. Do you know what they were doing, Harper?"

I swallow my water and look up at my father towering above me. He scares me. For the first time in my life, he scares me. "I don't know."

"We need to move," he says, finally answering my question about the ship. "Her body wasn't found and it hasn't washed up. But we can't risk searching anymore. So it's better to get out into international waters in case the local authorities come asking questions." He places a bottle of pills on the table. The orange bottle with the white top the same size and shape as all the others he's given me over the years.

"I'm not taking those," I say, immediately pulling myself together.

"No?" He walks back over to his seat just as the servers come in and place a covered plate in front of him. One is placed in front of me as well, and then the two servers remove the silver domed tops at the same time to reveal shark steaks, rice pilaf, and two slices of lime. "You've said that before, darling. But you know the pills help. So why deny yourself?"

I just stare at him. *Deny* myself? That's an unusual way to put it.

"I'm not going to make you do anything, Harper. You're a grown woman now. I've already stated, you're not a prisoner."

"Then let me go."

"We're out to sea."

"We have a tender."

"Yes, but it's in need of repair. Which is why Tet had to hire a boat to bring you out to the ship."

I stop listening and instead take my attention to my food. I'm starving and there's no way in hell I could resist this meal. I don't know how many days I've really missed, but it's several by the pain in my stomach. I cut the tender shark steak with my knife and start shoveling it into my mouth. Aside from that one nice dinner with James, I haven't had many decent meals since I left home.

"So," my father continues, "now that you're safe and Tet is off looking for your brother so he can bring that file to me, I'd like to make you a proposition."

I stop chewing and just stare at my plate. And then I regain my composer and swallow. "What kind of proposition?"

"Your promise."

I look up at that and my father tisks his tongue. "No, Harper. Darling. You were not promised to Tet. Please have more faith in me that that. Why would I give you to a demented killer?"

I have no idea. "Then who?"

"No one on the ship that night. He's a secret. A secret so powerful it will rock this Company to the core. You see, Harper, regardless of what most people think, I'm not the head of this organization. I'm just a convenient figure our enemies can focus on when they feel the need for revenge. I'm… a distraction. The real power belongs to someone else."

"Who?"

"You'll see."

"What do you think James will do when he figures this out? And what if I'd prefer James over this… new person?"

"Harper. I know you think I'm out to get you, but I'm only trying to keep you safe."

"Like you kept my mother safe?"

His expression hardens immediately. "Do not mention her again."

"Why, because you let her be killed?"

He pounds his fists on the table, making all the silver jump. I jump as well and I find myself scooting back from the table, ready to flee. But then I realize I'm on a fucking ship. There's nowhere to go.

"Dinner's over." And then he stands up and walks a few steps before turning back to me. "Don't forget your pills, Harper. The deeper you dig, and the more you want to know, the more likely you are to take them."

TWELVE

Harper

"I'm not done," I tell the server who comes to take my plate. I will be damned if I will be sent back to my cabin like a child when I'm still hungry. "Bring me dessert and then leave me alone to eat in peace."

"Yes, ma'am," the server closest to me says. And then with a nod, she signals her co-worker and they walk away.

I eat every last bite of my shark steak, most of the rice, and the dessert—which is apple cobbler à la mode.

I let out a long sigh.

OK. So my father is still a prick and he's got the upper hand. I'm stuck on this ship and I have no idea what he's doing or where we're going. But… I have to think up a *but*, because I need one right now. I need some inner reassurance that this is not over yet.

But. I'm not that weak and scared little girl who left here last year. I'm different. And I don't believe half that stuff he says about James. I accept that James can't be all there. He's responsible for too many atrocities to not be affected by it.

But James was lucid and in control one hundred percent of

the time we were together. Isn't that all that matters? He was not indecisive or confused. So even if some of that stuff is true about his psyche, does it matter if it doesn't affect him in his day to day life?

But Harper, the reasonable me points out. *You were only really with him for a few days. It's one small snapshot of who he is.*

True. But he was always thinking of us.

Except he killed Sasha.

That makes me bring my napkin to my mouth to stifle my shock.

How? How could he do that? We were only together for a short while, but we were like family. Why would he bother to care about her if his objective was to shoot her in the end? I don't understand that.

God, I wish I had a friend to talk to.

My mind immediately goes to the phone. I want to text him so bad.

I get up and go back to my room to change. The phone is still there. Right where I left it. I pick it up and find the message.

I'm sorry.

I can't stop myself. I text back. *Why? Just tell me why you're doing these things.* I press the send button and watch the little green bar as it tries to send my message. It fails and then the message string disappears. Dammit. I key in James' number and rewrite the text, pushing send again. I repeat this process and press send several more times before I understand that we're out to sea and my phone won't work.

"Score one for Dad," I mumble, throwing the phone down on the bed.

But I'm not going to sit in my cabin and mope, that's for sure. So I put on a pair of clean shorts and a tank top, then slip on my flipflops and go back above deck. When I get to the party area, I plop down on one of the couches and tuck my feet up underneath me.

"Jesus Christ, Harper, what the fuck is happening?"

"I had no idea your mouth was so filthy. Your father never mentioned that."

I stand up so I can see over the dining table. The direction the unfamiliar voice came from. "Excuse me?" I don't see anything beyond but the empty deck and the black sky.

"Sorry," a man says, standing up from the hot tub on the outer deck. The thick muscles of his chest drip water as he steps out, and then he smiles at me, just as he grabs one of the large white towels with the ship's name monogrammed on them. He drags it across his face and chest and then tosses it aside.

I have lost my mind. My heart shudders and then stops. I have to sit down quickly because I know without a doubt I am going to faint.

Strong hands catch me just before I fall and lay me down across the couch cushions. "Sorry. I didn't expect to see you up here so soon after dinner. This wasn't the way I wanted us to meet."

I sit up because I feel like I'm suffocating. His touch sends chills up my spine and I put a hand up to push him away.

I meet his eyes briefly and my head spins.

"James?" I know it's not him, but I can't stop myself from asking. "James? Is that you?"

The man who looks like James, but who I know is not James, shakes his head. "No, sweetheart. I'm Vincent." He smiles at me and there's a twinkle in his green eyes that makes me hold my breath again. "The control."

THIRTEEN

Harper

"I don't understand." I'm breathing all heavy and wrong and he's still touching my arm. I shake off his hand and pull away. "I don't understand."

The man who looks like James sighs. "OK. Let me start from the beginning. In a science experiment you have three variables. You have the product, the reactant, and the control."

"What?"

"I was told you were quick."

I squint at him. What the fuck is he talking about?

"OK, a product is—"

"I know what a fucking control is. What I don't know," I seethe, "is why the fuck you look like *James*."

He reaches over and I recoil and scoot back until I'm pressed up against the couch cushions. His fingertips touch my cheek and then drag down until his hand flips over and his knuckles slide under my chin. He gently tips it upward. "Calm down for me, please. And I'll explain."

"This is me being calm," I say back, still angry.

He smiles and drops his hand. “James is my brother.”

“He never said he had a twin.”

“He doesn’t know he has a twin.”

“I don’t understand.”

“Harper, work with me here, darling. OK?” He pauses like I’m supposed to take that opportunity to agree with him. “I didn’t expect to see you tonight. Your father said—”

My father *knew* about this.

“—you’d go to your room after dinner. So I took this opportunity to relax. I live in a stressful world, as you do, I’m sure. And I wasn’t thrilled that I had to be the one to have this conversation with you. I didn’t feel it was my place. Your father should’ve cleared all this up last year—”

Oh my God. What is he saying?

“—but since you’ve seen me now, I guess I’ll just have to do my best.”

I stand up, shaking my head. “No.”

“Sit down, Harper.”

“No,” I say again, stepping away from the couch. He stays where he is so I walk all the way to the edge of the living room. “I know what you’re going to say and I don’t believe you.”

“It’s true, Harper. I’m your promise, not James.”

“No. I belong to him. He said so.”

“James is delusional. Besides, I don’t see you as property, so I’m very unhappy that he made you believe you were one of his belongings.”

“Who the fuck are you?”

“Vincent. Fenici.” He says it very slowly, like I’m incapable of understanding what’s going on.

I do understand. I just don’t want to believe it.

“James and I are twins. When we turned sixteen, we were brought to an island to meet you. Not together, of course. We lived separate lives since shortly after our second birthday.”

“I didn’t see you there.”

He chuckles. “Of course you did, darling. We spent the day together. I watched you blow out your candles. I gave you a gift before I left. Some colored pencils to draw in the notebook that James gave you.”

I have to hold on to the edge of the bar to steady myself. "James was with me that day, not you."

"Sorry, sweetie. That was me. James said no to the Admiral's offer. He was sent on his way that afternoon. I spent the rest of the day with you. Not him."

That's not right. James had that notebook all these years. He stole it back. So he was *there* that night. But this guy… this Vincent… he was the one I was with? I think my world is tipping. No. I think my world is capsizing.

"Are you OK?"

I swallow hard and look over at the man who is not James. What the hell am I supposed to feel about this? "I'm promised to you, not him?"

"Me," he says. "Not him."

I stare at him in the dim lights from the overhead canopy. Candles flicker on the tables and the fire warms one side of my body, while the ocean spits up a spray that cools the other. "What if I don't want you? What if I want him?"

"He's dead, darling."

"He's not dead!" I scream it. My whole body begins to tremble and before I know it, I'm shaking uncontrollably. "He's not dead!"

"He might as well be. He's insane, and that is an indisputable fact. Harper, listen to me. Ask yourself this question. Who the hell kills their own brother? A brother they were not even angry at. A brother they loved and grew up with. A brother who saved their life as many times as they saved his. Their partner. Who kills their *partner*?"

"He told me why he did it and I agree with him. He had a good reason."

"Why?" the man who looks like my James demands. "Tell me why he did it, then."

I think of what James told me in the desert bathroom the other day. About Tony's girlfriend and baby. He did it to keep the baby safe. But if no one knows there's another Company kid running around, I'm not gonna be the one to spill the beans. "It's private," I say.

"It's not private, Harper. We know about the child. And she's going to be brought back into the fold. Soon. Once we settle who is in charge of things."

"I have no idea what you're talking about." My face is devoid of emotion. No expression at all. I put on the best liar face I have.

Vince smiles and shrugs, letting it drop. "Do you want to come sit with me?" he asks.

I shake my head no. "I'm going to bed."

"Not yet, Harper. Come here, please. Sit across from me, because we need to talk before you go back to your room and get your things."

Get my things? "What?" Oh, shit. My heart is pounding in my chest.

"Come sit. Please."

I do go sit because I need the three moments it takes to cross the room in order to think. He's taking me somewhere. I need to get my things.

I settle on the couch across the long glass coffee table from him and try to stop my knees from knocking together. I almost wish I could have a pill.

"You were promised to me on the day you turned six. It was an agreement of the highest importance because it bonded your family to mine. Like in the old days when a princess was married off to an enemy's prince."

"Are you the enemy?"

His smile gives me the chills. "In a way. But so is James. We come from the same Company family. Understand this. I am no different than him in that respect. So please"—he stops to smile—"don't be frightened. I'm sure you are far more dangerous than I am."

"What's your job?"

He hesitates, but the smile never wavers. "It's a new position, actually. For a new era in the Company business. Aaaand I'm not sure how much you know, but I'm sure you understand why I can't divulge everything."

Still with the smile.

"What's that mean?" I decide dumb questions are best with this guy. He likes to feel superior. Why not lure him into his comfort zone?

"It means you don't need to worry about it. Now, let's talk

logistics, OK? I'm here. You're here. We're talking. The inevitable has been discussed. So even though you were scheduled to leave with me tomorrow, the helicopter is ready and waiting. So I think it's better for you that we leave tonight. What do you think, Admiral?"

I turn around and find my father standing behind me. Smiling.

"Harper. I'm sorry I kept this from you. It would've probably saved thirteen lives had I just been upfront about who your promise was. But it was a difficult thing to consider. It was a difficult conversation to have."

"But now you're fine with me being given to some stranger?" I snap. "I'm just supposed to leave with him? Right now?"

"You already liked him as James, Harper. He *is* James, only better."

"In what way? The way he talks down to me like I'm a baby? The way he gives me the chills that makes me want to avoid touching him? Or the way he—"

"That's enough," my father barks.

It stops me cold. I've lived with that shout my whole life. I can't stop my immediate reaction to be quiet.

"That's enough now. James is psychotic, Harper. He will kill you or he will get you killed. He's not safe. He's not family material. He's not father material. We've dispatched a team to follow him and take him out. If they haven't killed him yet, they will. Very soon. He's as good as dead. So the sooner you accept the fact that Vincent is your promise, that Vincent is the man who loves you above all others, that Vincent will keep you safe, the sooner you can move into your new life."

"What life? If I'm his property, then what life?"

"Children, Harper. Your job as a Company woman is to have children. And"—the Admiral looks over at Vincent and smiles—"Vincent says he'd like you to take part in his new role as well. See? He already loves and cares for you enough to consider the idea of letting you work."

"Letting me—" I can't think straight. "Children?" He has got to be joking. "Slaves, you mean? Like me? Daughters who will be sold off when they turn eighteen? Sons who will be given away to whomever to be turned into killers?"

"Your sons will not be killers, Harper. Don't overreact. Your sons will be Company royalty."

"Like Nick?" I scoff. "Who was taught to kill and taught me to kill?"

"Nick," my father laughs. "Nick is not royalty, sweetie. You are not royalty. But your children, with Vincent's blood mixed in, will be. You are the start of a new Company line. The two strongest families will be united after tonight and a new era of power will begin. We own everything, Harper. We have people in positions in every world government that matters. We run the US Senate and the next president will be a Company man, regardless of which party gets elected. We hold private utility companies, prisons, water treatment plants, hospitals, and millions of acres of farmland. We control everything but the hearts and minds of the people. And that comes next. You, Harper, along with Vincent, will capture their imaginations. The pretty girl with the handsome politician. The road to power, and your place in history, is my everlasting gift to you."

Oh my God. It's like he's a villain in those comic books Nick and I used to read.

"Ready?" And then Vincent has me by the elbow. Not hard, still gentle. But it's not even a question. It's a foregone conclusion.

I let him lead me away, not knowing what else to do.

"Harper," Vincent says as he leans down in my ear. "Do you want anything from your room?"

I consider this. I consider the phone. But the more I think about it, the less likely it is that the phone in my room is the phone I had from before. I probably fucked things up by trying to text James. "No, thank you," I say, falling back on my manners to help me get through things.

My promised man wraps an arm around me and guides me over to the ladder that leads below deck. "I thought there was a helicopter?" But before the words are out of my mouth, I know there's no helicopter waiting on this ship. It's a fucking sailboat.

"Once we board my yacht we can take the helicopter to my home. *Our* home," he amends. It will be wonderful, you'll see. And soon, Tet will be gone and you'll never have to think of him again."

He pulls a hoodie on over his head and then he slips his feet into a pair of gray canvas boat shoes and grabs my hand. We go down three floors and make our way to the garage. There are men there waiting for us. My body feels hot as I realize that they all knew I was coming aboard only so I could be given away. They probably love the fact that I'm being punished. I killed thirteen people, some of them crew. They probably hate me.

"Step carefully," Vincent says as he holds his hand out to help me into the tender, but not ours. His.

I settle in the seat next to Vincent at his request and he puts his arm around me. "Are you cold, lionfish?"

"What did you just call me?" The nerve of him.

"Lionfish," he says, nuzzling my ear as we take out into the darkness. "Remember I gave you that name on the beach? After you told me about touching the stingers?"

"I told that story to James, not you."

"Baby," he says as his hand slips between my legs and his mouth covers mine for the briefest of moments. "I am James. How do you not recognize me?"

I tilt my head up to say no, but his mouth is right there. It covers mine. His tongue slips in and tangles with me. His hands are busy rubbing my inner thighs and then his fingers slip right up to my panties.

I push him off and scoot away. "You're not him," I say, not very convincingly.

"Oh, but I am. And when we get home, we're gonna have that talk about power all over again."

FOURTEEN

Harper

He is not James. He is not James. He is not James.

I know he's not James, I don't need the mantra to convince myself. I say it because I need to keep my mind from spinning out of control while we're on the boat. It takes a long time to reach his yacht, and once we're there, he takes me to a stateroom and says good night.

That's it. Just good night.

The closet has two outfits. One set of modest night clothes. Tank top and shorts. And one set of outdoor wear. Jeans, boots, plain cotton shirt, and a light jacket.

I have a feeling we're not going to be staying on board the yacht very long.

The bathroom is fitted with a large round tub, and even though all these things have happened to me in such a short time, I soak in the tub. I need something to settle me. To calm me. Hot water and a bottle of pills in an orange bottle on the counter are all I have, and I don't want to take those pills. I cannot take those pills again.

So I soak for a little while and then change into my night

clothes. When I come out of the bathroom, there's a tray with cocoa and cookies.

Cocoa and cookies. Like I'm six fucking years old.

I drink the cocoa and skip the snack, then climb into bed. The ship is moving fast—full speed from the feel of it. It makes my stomach sick to think about it. It's been far too long since I've been at sea for this to feel normal, but after tossing and turning for a few minutes, I finally drift off.

Sometime later Vincent wakes me. It takes me several seconds for his face come into focus once I open my eyes. "We're ready. Please get dressed." The hand he places on my arm gives me the chills and I pull away. The bedside light is flicked on and I have a chance to get a good look at him before he leaves my stateroom.

Why does he have to look exactly like James?

I dutifully put on the clothes and exit the cabin.

Vincent is waiting for me in the hallway wearing a dark blue suit with a tie that matches. Gone are his hoodie and boat shoes. He looks like a businessman now instead of a beach bum.

He gives me a quick smile and then I'm ushered up to the helipad and into the waiting 'copter before I even have time to think. I don't know how long I slept, but it feels like late evening now. Almost all day if I had to guess.

Did he drug me? With the cocoa?

I don't ask where we're going. I stopped talking to him after he said he was James. I mean, please. These people treat me like I'm an idiot. He thinks I don't know the difference between a stranger and the man I'm in love with?

God, did I just admit I love James?

I turn my head in the 'copter so the impostor can't see me, and I grin. I've barely spent any time with James at all, but I know what I feel, and it's love.

I miss him so bad.

Why did he drop me off?

I mean, yes, I can follow the logic. He was probably freaked out when that guy drugged me and maybe he thought I'd be safer on the yacht.

I probably *would* be safer on the yacht.

But I'm not on the fucking yacht. I'm in a goddamned

helicopter flying to God knows where. And all this stuff about James being crazy—yeah, I can see that too. He's totally psycho. I grin again. But that's just part of his charm.

What girl does not fantasize about taming a wild man? Well, I never have until now. But that's how I feel about it. James Fenici is one of the most dangerous men in the world and he wants to take care of me. He wants to love me and sleep with me. He listens to what I have to say and he puts all the violence aside when I'm next to him.

Grown men are terrified of him. Global organizations haven't been able to kill him. And yet when his cock is in my mouth, he gives me all the power.

I could get drunk on that power I have over him. I could get off on that power too.

I want *my* James.

I'm not even remotely interested in what this stranger who looks like him has to say about anything. I don't care if he's the one I was promised to. What kind of man accepts a six-year old girl as his wife?

Sick. That's sick.

James was the one who said no. James was the one with integrity. James was not insane when we turned six that year. He was untouched by all the killing that came afterward. And he was taken prisoner that first year. Left somewhere horrific for a long time, the notebook said. That's bound to change anyone. And that's not his fault.

The helicopter finally starts to descend just as the sun begins to set and even though I must've slept all day, I'm so tired.

"We're about to land." Vincent's voice crackles though my headpiece.

I look over at him and before I can stop myself, I smile. His face catches me off guard a little. I mean, they are identical. The eyes. The haircut. The broad shoulders that taper down to the perfectly proportioned waist.

"I hope you like it."

I cut the smile and add a nod. What does he want me to say? I'm not staying here. I'm not gonna be his wife. I do not give a shit what promise was made. I belong to someone else.

A few minutes later and we are on the ground and everything becomes all rush, rush. I have never understood the hustle involved with boarding and disembarking a helicopter. Why must they pull me along like we're in some kind of war zone?

I go with it. Vincent's grip on my arm is tight. Tighter than is normal. And I wonder how worried he is about me running off into some unfamiliar woods as he drags me away from the rotating blades and ushers me up a series of steps that lead to the back patio of an imposing Mediterranean-style mansion.

Even though the Spanish tile roof and warm stucco exterior might look welcoming in bright sunshine, the dusk makes it look ominous. "Where are we?" I finally ask as we slow our pace and he straightens out his shirt collar.

"North of Santa Barbara."

"How the hell did we get to Santa Barbara from Newport Beach in a sailboat?" More importantly, how will James find me here? I'm not all that up on my American West Coast geography, but I think that's a fair distance.

"We motored up the coast," he answers back. "It's difficult to navigate up the California coast in a sailboat."

"We must've been hauling ass."

"Language, Harper," he says, only half paying attention as he reaches for my hand.

I shake it off. "Don't," I growl at him. "I might be your prisoner for now, but I'm not your fucking child to admonish."

He snatches my hand and yanks me into his chest. "Manners, Harper Tate." His steely gaze transfixes me. His green eyes flash. "I was told you have them. Was I lied to?"

I match his gaze and refuse to bend. "I *have* manners. But I'm not sure you deserve them."

He loosens his grip on my hand and exhales. "Please," he says, pressing his fingertips to the space between his eyes like he has a headache. "I don't like the language and I don't like the attitude. We're both tired. We've been through a lot. And we're going to freshen up and have a nice dinner so we can chat."

"If you're still insisting you're James, then I'm going to refuse that chat."

He grits his teeth. "If James is the one you think you want, then

I *am* James."

"How did you know about that conversation we had about power?"

He laughs a little under his breath and then leans into my ear. "I was there, Harper. That was me."

"That was not you!"

"How do you know?"

I just stare at him. "I know."

He moves my hand to the bulge between his legs and presses it. "Tell me how you know."

I yank my hand away and step back. "You were watching us. You had cameras. Something. But that was not you. And I'll tell you how I know. Because even though James made it very clear I belong to him, he does not treat me like property. He respects me."

"Ha," Vincent laughs. "That's a good one. Well, you got me. I'm Vincent. I'm not sorry for being Vincent instead of James. I am sorry I didn't get to you before he did. I am sorry you sucked his cock before you'll suck mine. But we have all the time in the world to make up for that."

I can't even move, that's how off-guard I feel. Should I fight him? But where would I go? I don't even know where I'm at. Santa Barbara. I'm just not sure where I could go from there.

His hand wraps around my waist, squeezing as he pulls me close to his chest. "Forget about James, Harper. James is a dead man. He's crazy, OK? He's lost touch with reality. He kills people for no reason anymore. He's hunted down all his friends in the Company and tried to kill them, one by one. We've known this for almost a year now. And the only good thing he's done since then is kill our brother, Tony. Because Tony was just as certifiable as James."

"It's not his fault he was forced to kill people for a living. It's not his fault the Company turned him into that."

"Harper," Vincent whispers. "Listen to me. It *is* his fault. He was the favorite, Harp. Our parents loved James above everyone. I didn't grow up in the same house, but I knew who he was. Our father pinned all his Company hopes on James. All he had to do was go to that beach when you turned six and say, *Yes, Admiral. I'll take her.* And his life would be mine. And my life would be his.

You'd be in love with me right now if he said yes, because I would be the one who went crazy and found you on the beach."

"But he didn't say yes. You did."

Vincent pushes me away and takes a step back. "You're wrong. I never got asked. I told you, I was the control. I didn't participate in anything. I was secluded from the Company. I was raised like any other rich American boy. I never killed anyone. I never went on missions. I just existed. I have an impeccable record. A paper trail that can be followed from the time I turned sixteen until now. So when the vetting begins for the multiple political offices I will hold, I appear untouched. Perfect. The perfect man. Raised in the perfect home. Wedded to the perfect woman who has no record at all. Who was raised on a fucking boat in the middle of the ocean. Who never went to school. Who never had her picture taken and plastered all over the society pages. You," he whispers, "are the perfect blank canvas."

He gives me that hard stare again and this time it doesn't make me defiant, it makes me curious. "What do you want from me?"

"I want what I was promised."

"I never made a promise to you."

"You think you love him, but you don't know him. You know *me*."

"You're not the guy I spent time with, Vincent."

"I'm the guy from your birthday party, Harper. I'm the guy you fell in love with." He slowly moves his hands up towards my face and cups them around my cheeks. "I deserve the same chance you gave James. That's all I'm asking for. Be fair, Harper. You don't know me yet. I'm not going to hurt you. I just want my chance."

FIFTEEN

Harper

He won't let go of my face and I can't stop looking into his beautiful green eyes.

Why? Why does he have to look like the man I love?

"Just a chance, Harper. That's all I'm asking. I'll make a deal with you, OK? I won't push you. I'll give you some space and some privacy. I'll give you freedom in the house. I will even give you a phone to call the man you think you love."

I take in a deep breath at that offer.

"I know you want to talk to James. I understand. If you give me a few days with no fighting and no rebellion, then I will let you call him."

"Why not now?" I know I'm pushing it, but what kind of killer would I be if I didn't?

Vincent sighs, but he doesn't immediately say no and that gives me hope. "If I let you call James now, you'll be good for me? You'll give me a chance?" He stares down into me. His hands soften against my cheeks.

"Right now?"

"A real chance."

"OK," I say warily. Is Vincent for real? Or is this some kind of trick? "If you let me call him, I'll give you a chance."

"One call. Twenty seconds. You can't tell James you're with me, where you are, or what we're doing. You can't be upset. It's one call just to hear his voice. And if he doesn't answer, he might be dead. If he doesn't answer, you will *assume* he is dead. You will drop it and focus on your life here with me. I'll give you one act of trust on my part if you make this promise to me. Because I'm certain of one thing, Miss Tate. He's not the man you are meant to be with. That's me. So go ahead. Call him."

Vincent reaches into his jacket and pulls out a phone. He swipes his fingers across the screen to wake it up and then presses an app on the home screen. "This reroutes the call so it looks like it's coming from another number."

I press in the numbers and listen to it ring.

"Harper…"

I take a deep breath to stop myself from crying so Vincent isn't tempted to end the call if James thinks I'm upset.

"Harper? You there?"

I swallow hard and nod. "They said you were dead!"

He laughs. "Fuck. I'm fine. They're amateurs. It's you I'm worried about."

"Why did you drop me off, James? I don't understand what I did wrong."

He hesitates. "You have to trust me, baby. Do you trust me?"

A tear slips down my cheek but Vincent reaches out to swipe it away. "Yeah." I breathe through my pent-up sobs. "I do. I can't talk. I just wanted you to know I love—"

I get the three beeps that tell me the call has been dropped and I look down at the screen as the app flashes a no-signal icon at me. "We got cut off."

"I'm sorry," Vincent says. "I'm sorry it was short. But do you feel better now?"

I give his phone back and turn away. When he reaches for my hand I let my fingers slip into his because I'm lost all of a sudden.

James.

Just hearing his voice shakes me up. He does that to me. He

shakes my foundation and rocks me to the core. He can calm me down and light me up in the same breath. He's the only person on this planet I need right now. He's the only person on this planet who makes sense.

And when I look up into the green eyes of the man who says I belong to him, I get lost in them. My world spins. My reality is shattered. The muscles in my legs get weak and then my knees buckle and I'm falling. Falling into the arms of the man who wants me to be his.

Why does he have to look just like him?

"I've got you, Harper."

But the wrong man scoops me up and cradles me in his arms. The wrong man whispers comforting reassurances in my ear. The wrong man sits down on an outdoor couch and holds me tight until I stop shaking.

"It's the drugs. Just relax and let it wear off."

I push off him until he lets me go and then I get to my feet. "I'm fine," I say, refusing to meet his gaze. "I just need to settle in."

"You're not fine, Miss Tate. But I agree. The sooner you can settle in, the better off you'll be." Vincent gets up and leads me into the home through a massive set of French doors. We end up in a living room. Or maybe it's a ballroom. It's so big it makes me dizzy when I look up at the ceiling. We're entering through the back of the house, so we're facing the back of the stairs. Up above is a long balcony that spans the entire length of the room. There are two hallways on either side of the stairs, both on the upper and lower floors. Like this house has wings to it.

"Come, I'll take you to your room. Do you need me to carry you? Or can you manage the stairs?"

What a ridiculous question, I think as I follow him to the stairs. But I'm only halfway up before my pace slows from exhaustion.

"You need to take it slow, Harper. You've been drugged too many times in the last several days." And then he scoops me up in his arms and takes the remaining steps with ease.

He sets me on my feet again when we get to the top and retakes my hand to lead me off to the left. We walk to the very end of the wing and stop in front of a set of double doors. "This is my room," he says as he opens the door and waves me in. "You can stay in here and I'll sleep in my office."

I look back down the hallway. "Why can't I have my own room?"

"Because this *is* your room, lionfish."

"Don't call me that," I growl. "And I don't want to stay in your room. It's uncomfortable."

"We can change it tomorrow. But all your things are in here. So for tonight, this is your room."

"I don't have any things," I snap. I can't help it. I'm tired and I'm starting to feel sick. Probably from all the drugs, as he so thoughtfully reminded me.

"This whole place is filled with your things, Harper. It's a Company house built for us. Let me show you your closet so you can choose a dress for dinner."

Dinner? Fuck. I cannot do dinner. Please, no. "Can't I eat in my room?"

"No," he says kindly but sternly. "It's better for you not to have too much time alone to think. Especially when you haven't taken your pills."

I scrunch up my eyes. "I don't take those anymore. James doesn't want me to take them."

"I don't want you to take them either, Harper. I want you to be in control at all times. I don't even want to offer you a drink at dinner, but my mother insisted we have a drink to celebrate."

"Your *mother*?"

My repulsion must be evident in my voice, because he chuckles. "Don't worry, she's not here. We'll have plenty of time to get to know one another before I unleash that horror on you."

I can't stop the huff of relief and then a smile follows before I can stop it.

"See," Vincent says. "See, it's not so bad here. Now look," he says, leading me into the massive room. The decorations are as traditional as the ones downstairs. The wood is dark and thick. The fabrics are rich colors—blood-red maroons, deep mustard yellows, and emerald greens. The drapes are closed tight so there's no view outside. But the windows must be spectacular, since the curtains flow down the entire length of the wall and spill out into a puddle of fabric on the floor. There's a sitting area on the far side of the room. It's bigger than the size of my living space in Huntington Beach. "Here are the closets," Vincent says, leading me over to another side of the room. "Mine is on this side and yours is over there."

He opens the double doors that lead to my closet and reaches around the corner to flip on the light. It's filled with clothes and shoes. Handbags. I've never carried a handbag. Boots. Not the kind you wear on a boat. The tall kind. The short kind. The fancy kind. There are so many cabinets and drawers, I have no idea what to think.

"Six," I say.

"What?" Vincent laughs.

"Six outfits. I've never owned more than six outfits in my life."

"Oh, yes. I guess there's not a lot of room for so many things on a boat."

"Why do I need so many clothes? I'm not trying to be difficult, I just don't understand it."

His hands wrap around my waist and he pulls me into his chest. "Miss Tate, your life is about to change. One day—not today, or tomorrow, or even next week when we have our first party as a power couple—but one day you will have so many people to see, and so many things to do, that you will look at this closet and realize it's not enough. You have dresses for balls. For fundraisers. For stepping out on the town with your husband for drinks. You have shorts and bathing suits for the pool or the beach, or traveling to see your father on his yacht. You'll have coats and boots for braving the weather when you have to visit New York or Chicago because some aspect of the many, many boards of directors you will participate in require your personal attention.

"Your life will be filled with interesting people, and special dinners, and parties. You will see injustices in this world and want to rage against them. You will command people to help you do that, and you will change the future. You will shape the future, Harper. You will talk and people will listen. You will admonish bad behavior and practices will change. You will be a force, Miss Tate. You will be a force and all those acts require clothes."

I try to picture myself as this person he describes but I can't. I try to picture myself in the future and find that I can't do that either. I don't think I've ever thought about my future.

"Clothes make you feel things, Harper. And right now I need you to choose a dress for me. Something that will make you feel something tonight. I don't want you drugged, or silent, or stupid. I want you to be you. So I filled your closet with every outfit I could get my hands on to give you a way to find yourself. So choose, Miss Tate. Who do you want to be tonight?"

I can't stop looking at his face the whole time he's talking. I swear to God, I can't stop. And it's not because he looks like James anymore. It's not his green eyes and dark hair or the perfect body I know he's hiding under that suit.

It's because he paints a picture I've never considered before. Up until this very moment, my future was all about seeing Nick again. Or lying next to James in some small apartment as we fled from one danger after another. Or maybe, if I was really dreaming big, a home. Like the one Merc had in the desert. A place with comfortable couches and air-conditioning to take the edge off the heat. With soft sheets and picture frames filled with moments we wanted to cherish together.

Simple.

My life has always been simple.

And I'm not saying one is better than the other. I'm not really saying anything with my hesitation. I'm just… considering my options.

"I don't know," I finally say. "I really have no idea who I am, let alone who I want to be."

Vincent's face changes in my moment of realization. "I see. Would you like to hear my opinion on what's in your closet?"

I nod. Because I could really use some guidance right now and he's all I have at them moment.

"This," he says with a smile as his fingertips gather a piece of light green fabric, "is a beautiful dress. My favorite, in fact." He lifts the hanger off the rack so I can see the dress displayed.

It's very pretty. Not sexy. But sophisticated. The pale green reminds me of a honeydew melon. And it's more of a gown than a dress. A soft chiffon gown with a shirred empire bodice, and skirts that flow all the way to the floor, like a column.

"It's pretty."

"Yes," Vincent says. "But maybe tonight you just want to be comfortable?" He pulls out a t-shirt with some writing on it. Grunge-style. Little rips in the sleeve to make it looked well-loved and well-worn. And then he opens a drawer in one of the many cabinets and finds a pair of denim shorts. "This is what you usually wear, right?"

I smile a huff out a laugh. "Yeah. I'm not very fancy."

"So wear this to our first dinner."

I look up at him and smile. "What are you going to wear?"

"I look pretty good like this," he says, gesturing to his suit. "I like to be fancy. But if you choose comfortable, I'll change."

I sigh and turn back to the green dress. He's good, I realize. He's very, very good at this. Here I am wondering what he wants me to wear to dinner with him, when ten minutes ago I was angry about being forced to come stay at his house.

I don't know what to make of it.

"Harper," he says softly behind me. "It's not a big decision. Just match the clothes to your mood and purpose."

"What if I don't know what I feel? Or what I want?"

"Well, that's understandable. It takes time. I'm sorry I was harsh with you earlier. I've set things up wrong. I've set you up to be combative, and I apologize. I don't want to fight. I just want to get to know you. So decide how you want to feel tonight, right now. And then let the rest go. Just enjoy it for what it is. A dinner. With me."

"I want to see myself in that dress," I whisper. "I've never worn something so… grown up."

"Then put it on. And come downstairs. We'll eat outside since it's nice. I'll wait for you there."

And then he backs out of my closet and I stand stock still as I hear the door close to the bedroom.

I look at the clothes.

I replay his words.

I see his intentions.

And none of it scares me.

But that… scares me.

SIXTEEN

Harper

I don't recognize myself when I look in the mirror and it takes me several minutes of self-reflection to decide I'm not sure if that's good or bad. Of course, that's hardly self-reflection. Usually when one self-reflects, they come to a conclusion. I don't seem to be able to come to any conclusions.

I sigh at my image. I'm happy with the way I look. I am a bit on the athletic side. My legs are muscular, but the dress falls all the way to the floor, so they can't be seen. My arms are a little too defined for a girl. But they are bronzed from the summer sun and the hairs on them are all that bleached shade of yellow that reminds me of Nick. His facial hair is like that.

God, I miss him. Does he know where I am? How will he find me now? My one-year anniversary is pretty much up. In fact, it might even be the same day James promised to come back for me. But I'm here in Santa Barbara and the two most important people in my life will be looking for me in the wrong place.

I shake off the worries. I can't worry right now. I just need a breath. I just need a break.

I just need to figure out who this girl in the mirror is.

My attention goes to my hair. It's a little long since I don't do anything beyond combing it these days.

What am I talking about? I've never done anything beyond combing it.

My face has that just-washed pink hue to it from scrubbing. I don't wear makeup, so I'm not sure if the way I look is acceptable or not.

And then the shoes. I have no idea what to put on my feet, so I put on some soft yellow ballet flats.

Will Vincent like my choice? Do I care if he likes it? Why the fuck am I wondering?

I turn away from the mirror and walk out of the closet. I'm done. It's a dress. It's a dinner. I've worn hundreds of dresses and attended just as many dinners.

I walk out of the room and make my way to the stairs. He said he'd be outside, so when I reach the bottom I walk around to the back of the house and squint my eyes as I try to find him through the glass doors. It's no use. The lights are on inside and out there it's dark. So I can't see through them.

I walk calmly to the French doors I entered in a little while ago and open them. There is no one on the terrace, but I see a flickering fire a little way past where the helicopter landed.

"Vincent?" I call.

No answer. But I can see a shadow in front of the flames. I could yell and make him acknowledge that it's him. Or I could just walk down there myself and stop being such a baby.

I have killed fourteen people, so I opt for being a grownup. But every step makes my heart beat erratically.

I'm more than halfway to the fire when he turns and yes, it is Vincent. My heart calms. Why? I'm not sure. This man took me away from everything I know and forced me into a life I neither asked for nor want.

Why am I such a nervous person? How can this stranger make me feel better so easily?

Am I drugged? I don't feel drugged right now. But pretty much everyone has admitted to drugging me recently. So hey, it's not an outlandish question. I should stop accepting drinks from these people.

"I love it," Vincent says as soon as I'm close enough for him to reach out and grab my hand. His eyes slowly track down my slim body and then come to rest on my breasts before he looks back up at my face. "You're stunning."

I want to smile with satisfaction for putting myself together properly, or maybe even from the praise and desire I hear in his voice. But I hold it in.

It's wrong. God, this is all so fucked up. "I think James would've liked this dress too." I say it to be spiteful.

But Vincent doesn't even blink. "I'm sure he would. As would any man, insane or not."

A dig. But a small one. Not one worth an argument. I don't care what Vincent thinks of James. I know James isn't insane when we're together, and that's all that counts.

"Ready to eat?" Vincent asks, after letting me pause to think about his remark.

"Where? I don't see a table."

He places his other hand over the small of my back to lead me towards a paved path. "There's a nice view of the ocean through these trees. I have an area set up down there that overlooks the marina and I thought it would be the perfect place for our first dinner."

We walk for a little ways in silence and then there's a break in the trees and sure enough, the moon is shining bright in the night sky, its reflection mirrored on the water below. The marina is small and so are the boats.

"It's a Company neighborhood, Harper. And the Company owns that marina too."

I'm not sure if he says it to just FYI me about how things are run around here. Or if he's cautioning me about trying to run away and ask for help. So I don't react.

"Here," Vincent says, pulling out a chair for me at a table set for two. "The servers should be here soon. But we can have a drink while we wait."

"I don't drink," I say as I place the white linen napkin in my lap.

"It's just a gesture, Harper. I'm sure your father gave you sips of champagne at dinner."

"Never."

Vincent sits across from me. The table is small, so he's close. Too close, I think. Too close for me to keep my distance from the way he's trying to make me feel. He's trying his best to make himself irresistible, and I'd like to try my best to resist him. But when I look across the table, I see James. His green eyes. His dark hair. His five o'clock shadow.

"Tonight will be your first, then," Vincent says, filling my flute with the light honey-colored liquid. It bubbles up, bursting into the air so that even from my seat I can smell the fruitiness of the vintage. He lifts his glass and holds it towards me. I reciprocate the gesture. "To all our firsts. I hope we have a lifetime of them."

I squint my eyes a little, but he pretends not to notice as he takes a sip. My glass is set back down with no drink.

"I prefer water, thank you. Do we have some water? In a bottle. With a sealed cap."

"Of course. The servers will bring it with the meal. Now tell me, do you like the dress? Because I like it very much."

"What do you like about it?" I'm genuinely interested.

"What's not to like?" he asks back with a chuckle. "The color makes you look like a woodland fairy. It plays against the amber of your eyes, making them look like two shining jewels. It shows off the curve of your shoulders. The bronze of your skin. And while it's sexy as all fucking hell, you're showing very little skin. This is a dress I'd take you out in public in. A dress that would allow others to see your beauty without giving them too much of an eyeful. It is, in fact, perfect. Now that you're wearing it, of course."

"Wow. That is some line of bullshit you have there, Vincent. James would say, *Harper, you're just as fuckable with no clothes on. But this dress just makes me want to rip it off you.*"

Vincent stares at me.

I stare at him. I have to tuck my smile down, but he's not having any trouble keeping his at bay.

"Do you want me to treat you like James, Harper? Do you want me to fuck your face in a hallway?"

My whole body goes hot with embarrassment. I'd forgotten he said he saw that. "How do you know he did that? Were you stalking me?"

"No," he growls. "I was watching James, and James was watching you. He had that little scene on tape in his apartment."

I can't breathe. That's how much this stuns me. "He did not."

"It's still there now. He never cleaned the place. He's gone, Harper. He's lost it. He's careless and stupid and what he did to you"—Vincent stops to shake his head—"it was sick."

Sick. The word reverberates around in my head.

Am I sick because I was turned on from it?

I look down at my lap just as the servers appear from the path. There's a whole crew of them, which is weird since I didn't see a single soul either time as I walked through the house. They set down platters with covers on them. And the water arrives. A pitcher is placed on a side table, since the table is so small it really can't fit. They did *not* bring bottled water.

Two servers lift off our plate covers simultaneously and the rich aroma of lobster and butter fills my nostrils.

God, I'm famished. I practically salivate as I stare at the meal. The server attending Vincent places a bib around his neck, while the one attending me does the same.

When they're done, Vincent says, "Thank you," and they leave us alone.

I am hungry and I really do want to eat. But I'm still thinking about James having a video of me in that hallway.

"I'm sorry," Vincent says. His tone is hushed and the anger is gone. "I shouldn't have told you about the videos. I'm just tired of hearing about him. When you disappeared last year, Harper, I was lost. I mean, I understand that it's wrong the way they set us up like that. But I hit the jackpot with you. I wanted you. Want," he corrects himself. "I want you. And then your father told me I had to wait it out. They were keeping tabs on you, but no one was allowed to go in. I was reluctant. I was crazy with worry. But as the months passed you settled in. Nothing seemed to be happening. It really did appear that you wanted to be alone."

I look up at him, knowing where this is going.

"But then James showed up and I was livid. That he could walk into your life after I'd given you all that space, and take—" Vincent stops talking. He shakes his head and then he looks down at his food and begins to eat.

"Take what?" I ask.

"Never mind."

"My virginity?"

"No," he says, shaking his head. "Your self-respect."

SEVENTEEN

Harper

That stuns me silent.

Vincent eats a few more bites. In silence.

All I see in my mind's eye is James straddling my hips in the hallway as he positions his dick over my face.

Your self-respect.

"Fuck. I'm sorry. Again." Vincent reaches across the table and puts his hand on mine. "Are you OK?"

I nod. Smile. Nod again with a bigger smile. "Fine. It's just…" I need to change the subject. Like now. "I'm not sure what's going on here. Is there some sort of… contract?"

All my life my father has used that word. *The contract needs to be fulfilled. The contract needs to be negotiated. The contract has been violated.*

Violated. I have only ever heard that mentioned once and it was the day Nick left. Right before we turned eighteen.

Vincent squints his eyes at me. As if he's suspicious. And that immediately makes me suspicious. "What makes you say that?"

"Well, you say you're my promise. Aren't there contracts in

place for promises?"

"Harper," he says in a tone that comes off as admonishing. "Promising girls to men on their eighteenth birthdays isn't even legal. Why would we need a contract that can't be upheld?"

I can think of a dozen reasons right off the top of my head. But the most obvious is to hold it over someone when they screw up. *See*, one might say, *I have your daughter promised to blahedy-blah. That was a nice match, hmm? But if you don't fulfill your end of the deal, she gets a fifty-year-old pervert from this pile of filth here.*

"I dunno," I say instead. It's obvious there are things going on with this little… arrangement… that no one is going to tell me. I mean, come on. Vincent is identical to my dream guy, only he's not insane and he's not a killer. He's filthy rich, he's got some sort of sway in the Company, and if I'm his wife, I go from little girl to powerful woman in one breath.

It's like…

Wow.

His fingers stroke the underside of my wrist as he waits for me to finish, but the sudden tingle that runs through my body steals my words.

I look down at his touches and then look up at his brilliant green eyes. They are smiling. "Hmmm?"

I shake my head. "Nothing."

"Why do you look so flushed?" he prods.

He must know why because he takes it one step further and picks up a strawberry from the small bowl of fruit on the side of my plate and touches it to my lips. I open them, unsure what choice I have, and take a bite.

The juice drips onto my lips and then he stands up and leans over the table and licks it off.

I blink up at him.

And then his hands are on my face and his tongue is on my mouth. His tongue is sweet from the champagne, and gentle as he teases me to see how far I'll go.

I really don't want to go far at all, but the trouble is, I don't know how to say no. I have so little experience with men. James is the kind of guy who tells you want you need, even if you don't want it. And I like to follow orders. I do it automatically.

Vincent must know this. He's probably taking advantage of the fact that I'm so easily manipulated.

But as soon as that thought manifests, he pulls back. "What's wrong?" he says, leaning a little farther in so he can breathe the words into my ear. "You don't like it?"

I didn't have a chance to wonder if I *liked* it. "I'm sorry, I just... I just don't know what I'm supposed to be doing here." I inhale deeply and his scent fills my nose. It's something I've never smelled before. It makes my mind swirl.

He leans back and takes his seat again. "Eating," he says simply. "I thought you might like a bite of fruit before we started with the main meal."

I bite my lip a little. "It was the kiss, that's all. I'm not sure what I'm supposed to be doing when you kiss me."

This makes him chuckle and I hate myself for thinking it's a nice rumbling sound. I picture James making that same noise when I lie on his chest in bed. "You can kiss me back, Harper."

I press my lips together and swallow.

"You can tell me no."

I stare into Vincent's eyes. The eyes that remind me of James. How do two men look so much alike? And how is it fair that I'm having trouble understanding why this man, who looks exactly like the man I love, is not him? Especially when I ache so badly for his comforting touch and bossing ways. I don't like to be in control of things. I'm not good at it. I have panic attacks, and I don't think straight. I'm a fighter because I was conditioned that way by my brother. But that's just me on the outside. The girl on the inside is so very, very weak.

"I'm not very good at saying no."

"That's because you want to say yes, Harp."

The nickname jolts me out of my little trance. He's so familiar with me. "Did you watch me every year, like James did? Did you come for my birthdays and watch me from afar?"

"God." Vincent laughs louder this time. "I can't believe that freak did that shit. It's so sick."

"What?" I'm confused.

"Harper, he was stalking you all these years. Your father was paranoid that he'd just steal you away or kill you in your sleep."

"What? That makes no sense. James loves me. My father sent him a plane ticket to wherever we were anchored for the party. He was just never allowed to see me in person."

"Is that what he told you?" Vincent shakes his head. "No, baby, that's not what was happening. James has been obsessed with you since that first year. He turned down the offer and I became your promise. James went on to become Six. He was captured in some shithole of a country that same year. They tortured him, scarred up his body real bad—"

"Wait." I put up my hand. "He doesn't have any scars. I've seen his body and it's perfect."

Vincent's eyes narrow as he takes in the full meaning of my words. "Then you didn't look close enough. He was treated with lasers after One rescued him, but they were not completely removed." Vincent's expression falters and he frowns for a moment. "You know, I loved him. I might've never known him since we were separated when we were two years old. But I knew *of* him and I loved him. I missed him too. I'm sorry he had that life and I had this one. I'd have given this all up to be his twin. I'd even have joined him. I would've been Six Point Five if we were allowed. You should understand that, Harper. How a twin feels about their sibling."

And this I *can* relate to. I try and imagine my life without Nick. Nick, who protected me. Nick, who loved me unconditionally. Nick, who taught me to fight back and be strong. What kind of person would I be without Nick? "I'm sorry," I say. "I bet that was hard."

"It was. I don't relish the fact that you're mine and not his. I don't have any jealousy of him. Why should I, Harper? Why should I be jealous of him? I look exactly like him. I have the same features. The same intelligence. The same natural abilities. But he's so fucking damaged, you have no idea. He's not safe to be around. He's unstable in every sense of the word. He's got no loyalties, Harper. Don't mistake whatever you and he did together as meaningful. Because the Company has been watching him for more than a decade now. He takes women in every job. Befriends them. Fucks them blind. And then he kills everyone around them. And that's exactly what he's been doing with you."

I can't even breathe.

"He used you, Harper. He wanted that file you had to get even with your father for giving you to me. For making a mistake when he was sixteen that would change his life forever. He's never forgiven them for not rescuing him quicker even though he knew, if you fuck up a job, the only answer you'll get from the higher-ups is denial. He knew going in if he was captured he'd be left behind. And One risked his life to save him."

"So why has he been around so long? Why not kill him off ages ago?"

"Because he's efficient, Harper. You don't just train up a guy like Tet. All twenty-eight years of his life made him what he is. A killing machine. The perfect fucking assassin." Vincent leans over again, cupping my cheeks in his hands. "I need you to understand this, Harp. He's not the person you think he is. He's manipulative, calculating, and deadly. I can't blame you for falling for it. World leaders have fallen for it—"

My mind stops listening as I remember back when James was tallying up his kills back in the desert. Destabilized entire governments, he'd said. Too many to count, he admitted. What he did in Mexico counts as genocide.

He said it all right there. He told me everything Vincent is telling me now, only I never saw it clearly.

"—so don't think that you ever had a chance, Harper. Because you didn't. He's been planning this since that first year he went looking for you on your birthday."

"Planning what?" I ask, desperate to know what's really going on.

"To use you, Harper. He's going to kill your entire family, and he's gonna use you to do it."

EIGHTEEN

Harper

I think about this for a second. My first instinct is to defend James. He's not using me to get revenge. He's not using me to kill my family. He loves me.

But I can't bring myself to say it out loud and when I look Vincent in the eyes, he knows this. He knows I'm having doubts about James.

"Eat," Vincent finally says. "You're not eating."

"How can I eat when you just told me he's going to kill my brother and father?"

Vincent reaches over to stroke my cheek. "Harper, just let us take care of it, OK? We know Tet's plan. We know how he works. We know what he's after. So if you just trust us to take care of it, you will never have to think about him again."

"But every time I see you, I think about him. How can I not think about him when you're twins?"

"I'm sorry about that. I really am. We can talk about that later, when the timing is more appropriate. But for now, it's time to eat. You need nourishment."

Nourishment? Who talks like that? He sounds like my father—if my father ever cared that I wasn't eating. James would just say, *Eat your fucking dinner, and after we fuck, we can discuss.*

"Eat," Vincent repeats.

I pick at my lobster. I'm just not in the mood to put so much effort into a meal.

After watching me push my food around for a few minutes, Vincent sets down his fork. "You like lobster, Harper. I know you do. So what's the problem?"

"I'm not hungry anymore."

"You're going to eat. If you don't want this, then tell me what you do want."

I want James to be sane. I want James to love me. I want James to show up here and blow the place up and take me away. I don't even care where. Anywhere that's not here. Anywhere that's not filled with all this pretentious shit.

Lobster dinners? I think back to the many times I've had lobster. Lots and lots of times. It was something we ate regularly. Every couple weeks at least. But in Huntington I ate crap. For a whole year I got to choose my own food and I ate crap. And I ate it waiting for my brother to show up and save me from my dull life that scared me so bad I wanted to take pills to make the stress go away.

And then… James Fenici blew into my life and swept me off my feet. He demanded things of me. He had expectations. He had plans. And I loved that part about him. I loved that he drove a crappy Hummer. I love the fact that his go-to place was a shithole in the desert. I love the fact that no matter where we were, life was *real.* And exciting. I love that life with James is moment by moment. Nothing is dull or diluted. Life with James is a full-color, full-speed-ahead kind of life.

I fell in love with that man. I did. I fell in love with the James everyone else hates. And no amount of lobster dinners and Southern California mansions can compare.

I've had lobster dinners my whole life. I don't want lobster dinners. I want junk food. I want crap. I want all the things that make life feel good. I want all the stuff that's bad for me.

"Harper?" Vincent asks.

I look at him. Why does he have to look like my James?

"Harper, I'm not talking to myself. I asked you a question. Please respond with an answer. What do you want to eat, if not this?"

"I want… umm…" I don't even know how to explain. I don't even know if I want to explain it. Why bother? He's just going to get mad at me for wanting James.

"Want what, Harper?"

I shrug. "I want my life back. And my life isn't about lobster dinners anymore. It's about junk food."

Vincent just stares at me because I make no sense.

I tug on my lobster bib until it breaks and I drop it onto my plate. I look Vincent in the eyes as I push back in my chair and set my napkin on my lap. "I'm not hungry. I'm not eating. I'd like to go to bed if that's OK."

I expect him to get angry, but he surprises me with an understanding smile.

God, I can't take this confusion. I can't take it.

He takes off his bib and gets up and walks over to me, grabbing my hand in his. "OK."

And that's it. We start the walk back up the path to the house. Since we're facing it now, I can see it all lit up in the distance. It's massive, for sure. And overwhelming in its opulence.

Growing up on a yacht is a very luxurious experience, because let's face it, megayachts are pretty special. But no matter how big your ship is, it's never *big*. It's still a boat when you get down to it. It's still got a finite amount of space that everything has to fit inside.

So this mansion, to me, signifies wealth.

I grew up wealthy, but I didn't have a frame of reference to compare my life to except the local indigenous populations of the islands we frequented. They were poor, but think about it, we all lived in the same place. Paradise. We sat on the same beaches. We swam in the same turquoise blue ocean. My cabin was probably the same amount of square footage as the small bedrooms the other girls on the beach lived in.

We were not so different in my eyes. I'm sure their perspectives are different. But my perspective counts too. And that's what it was. So moving to the beach—into that small, cramped studio apartment—well, that was not so difficult for me. James' house in the desert, same thing. It was actually rather spacious. Not that we spent much time there. But it was comforting to have a small space with the open desert around. It mirrors the experience of our boat surrounded by the sea.

Merc's house? That was perfection. It was plain on the outside, but inside it was cozy and inviting. I've never met Merc, but he must be a pretty cool guy to have a home like that. It was like… a refuge.

I look up at the looming house before me and try to put the feeling it evokes into words. It's like… a citadel… a fortress. A—

"Harper?"

"Yes?" I answer to break up my thoughts.

"If you're not hungry for dinner, do you mind stopping in the kitchen to have a snack with me?"

When I look up, his eyes are soft and his mouth is turned up in a slight smile. "What kind of snack do you normally eat?"

"Hmmm." He thinks. "I'm not much of a snacker. I like meals. But I can bend, Harper. I'm not rigid. And maybe all you want is an apple? Or some crackers and cheese? There might even be some pastries."

I have to smile at that. I bet this guy never eats cookies from the looks of him. Sure, his body is pretty much the same as James'. But I'm sure James keeps trim from work. I bet Vincent keeps fit with diet and exercise like most people.

"OK. I am hungry, it's just—" My words fail me and I look around the massive living room as we walk through the French doors.

"It's just too much," Vincent says, leading me down a dark hallway.

"Yeah, it really is. I'm overwhelmed." We stop in an entrance and Vincent must find the light switch, because the blackness is suddenly illuminated. The kitchen is… industrial. Not warm and homey like the one at Merc's house. I'm disappointed.

"Look," Vincent says, looking down into an open bin built into the side of the wall. "Croissants?"

I make a face.

"Danish?"

A shrug this time.

He reaches down and pulls out a bag of rolls. "Bread and butter?" That makes me laugh because I know I'm being ridiculous and bratty. "I can throw in tap water if you want the real prisoner experience."

I frown. Because that's the word I was looking for outside as we walked towards the house. Not prisoner.

Prison. This place reminds me of a prison.

"Harper, just tell me what you want. I'll get it."

"James," I say before I can stop my mouth.

"Oh." He drops the rolls back into the drawer and closes it up. "OK. Well, I guess I'll just show you back to the bedroom and then I'm going to turn in. Maybe we can try again in the morning."

"Try what again, Vincent? What exactly do you expect of me? I'm in love with your brother. How can you possibly expect me to turn that off? Just because you look like him doesn't make you him. People aren't interchangeable. And I'm sorry you were the one promised to me. He was the one who found me. He was the one who came to me. He was the one who claimed me. And I let him. So no amount of wining and dining can make up for the fact that you came into my life too late."

He waves me back out into the hallway and turns the light off as we exit. The walk back to the bedroom is silent and heavy with regrets. I'm sorry I talked harshly to him and I'm sure he's sorry his brother beat him to the beach. But what can I do about this? I'm not going to give up on James before he even has a chance to talk to me about what these people are saying. That's stupid.

When we get to Vincent's bedroom, he walks in with me. But before I can protest about him spending the night in here, he puts his hand up. "Don't worry. I'm just grabbing clothes and then I'll leave you alone." And then he turns and walks into his closet.

A few minutes later he emerges with a handful of clothes and gives me a smile. "Good night, Harper. I hope you have a restful sleep." He pulls the door closed behind him and I'm alone.

I breathe a huge sigh of relief and strip out of my dress. I hang it up, admiring it as I put it back. It's very pretty. I should've looked at myself in the mirror more so I could remember it. I doubt I'll have a lot of dressing-up opportunities with James once he comes to take me back.

I shake away my melancholy thoughts and choose a tank top and a pair of soft shorts to sleep in. Once I wash my face and brush my teeth with a toothbrush fresh out of a package, I climb into the big bed. I expect it to smell like Vincent. His cologne. But it doesn't. It smells like laundry soap. He put fresh sheets on for me.

What a day, I think as I lay my head back into the soft pillow. My stomach is empty and rumbling, but my eyes are heavy and they win the war in the end. Because as soon as they close I'm dreaming of seeing Nick again. Of our birthdays coming up. Of Sasha and cozy homes in the desert like Merc's.

And of a life filled with James Fenici.

Because a life without him is not worth living.

There's no replacement for my James.

NINETEEN

Harper

When I wake up in the morning I have no idea what to do with myself. I realize, after lying in bed running all the past days' events through my mind, that I'm waiting for Vincent to appear and tell me what to do.

Just as this thought crosses my mind, the phone on the bedside table rings.

I stare at it. Do I answer it? I even look around, hoping Vincent will come rushing into the room, but he doesn't. I count the rings and when it gets to seven, I gather that it's not connected to a machine and pick it up just to make the noise stop. "Hello?"

There's a bunch of noise on the other end. "Harp?" Nick asks, sounding very distant.

"Nick? Oh my God, is that you?"

"It's me," he says over the roar of traffic. "It's me!"

"Where are you? How did you know I was here?"

"Vincent called me last night. He said you're having some trouble adjusting..."

I stop listening. Vincent called him? Called him? Like, just pressed a few numbers and presto, he's in contact with my brother who's been missing for a year?

"Harper?"

"Yeah," I answer. "Sorry, I didn't hear that."

"I said, he's worried about you. And how your time with Tet has affected you."

"My time with Tet." Nick's talking again, but I've tuned him out. He knew. He knew I was with James. And Sasha knew where he was too. He went to see Sasha. And my father knew James was with me, they were in contact and that's why James dropped me off at the ship.

"Harper? Are you still there?"

Somehow all these threads are connected. It's ragged, but somehow, everything is related. I just can't seem to figure out how.

"Harper!" He yells it this time.

"Sorry," I say back quickly. "I think I lost you for a second. The line went silent. Say it again."

"I said you have to stay away from Tet."

"Why?" My heart is beating so fast I have trouble breathing.

"Listen, Harp. Tet is on a mission, only he's not aware he's on a mission. They brainwashed him years ago, Harper. You need to stay far, far away from him, do you understand?"

"What mission?" I think I might get hysterical.

"I know you're not going to believe me, but he's been programmed. They're all programmed. Do you understand? All the assassins are programmed. They brainwash them when they're young. All growing up. They tell them things to make them loyal and then when they turn sixteen, the programming is activated and they become assassins."

"But you—"

"I was never programmed, you know that, *sister*. I was with you. We're different. We're the Admiral's children. We both have a role to play, but I don't have time to talk about that now. I got to get back on the road and I just needed to tell you that Tet is dangerous. I know you're probably wondering who to trust right now, but *sister*—" His formal use of sister makes me stop my panic and listen. It's how he always got my attention when we were young because he was not allowed to say my name in front of others.

Sister, he'd call me. It meant people were listening. "You have to trust me. Listen to Vincent. Please. He's telling you the truth. I'm on my way to see you."

"When?" I interrupt him. "When will you be here?"

"Two days, OK? Just hang in there for two more days and I'll explain. But for now, Harp, please—listen to Vincent. Give him a chance and let him take care of things. Just relax. You're safer now than ever before. You're safer with him than with your own father. OK?"

"OK," I say just to answer him. But he takes that as the end of our conversation and hangs up. The traffic noise cuts off and is replaced by silence.

I just stare at the phone.

My brother just called me. *Remember it all, Harper. Remember it all. Tet is brainwashed. Tet is dangerous. Tet is on a mission. Vincent is good. Nick will be here in two days.*

Sister.

That's the only word that counts.

I hang the phone up and practically collapse back into the pillows. Which parts are true? Which of the things he just told me are true and which are a cover for whatever it is he's planning?

I look over at the phone and sit up in bed with an idea. I can call James myself. I have his number. I reach for the receiver when there's a knock on the door.

Fuck. "Yes?"

It opens tentatively and Vincent peeks his head through. "I heard the phone. Who was that?"

"Nick," I say, swinging my legs over the side of the bed. Vincent eyes them for a moment before meeting my gaze. "He said you called him last night."

Vincent opens the door all the way and comes inside, closing it behind him. He smiles at me as he walks over to the bed and takes a seat. He sits close enough that our legs touch. "I did. I'm worried about you. I'm worried about Tet's influence on you. I'm worried about what he told you."

"Told me about what?"

"Anything. Everything. Everything he says is a lie, Harper. Everything. He can't help it. His life is all about lies. Lies keep him alive. He's nothing but the product of a dozen years of lies and secrets. He's killed hundreds of people. He's overthrown governments. He killed his own brother, for fuck's sake, Harper. That's got to bother you. Even if you think he had a good reason."

I start to say something, but I stop with my mouth hanging open. It makes me appear stunned instead of on the verge of defending him.

"I know," Vincent says, "it's horrific. It's horrible what they had him do. But Harper, he chose that life. You have to understand this."

"And you chose this one," I say flatly.

"I didn't choose. He did. He chose for me by choosing to be Six. I was always the control—"

"Wait. Control. Is that your code?"

"Code?" He looks at me funny.

"Your code. You know, from the Company."

"I don't know why you're talking about. I don't have any code."

Right. Secrets. But control. It's both a noun and a verb. And the way Vincent used it, it sort of means—

"Harper?" he growls. "Are you listening to me?"

Come can be a noun and a verb too, but—I have a private chuckle—the only noun it can be is semen. "I'm listening."

"What did Nick say?"

I eye him suspiciously. "You know what he said. You practically told him to call me and tell me these things."

"I told him to call you. That I was worried about Tet's influence. And I had every right to be worried, because yesterday, just before you called him, he tried to kill Nick by blowing up a cabin they were in."

I look away. "What?" He was with Nick? "Why would he do that?"

"He doesn't need a reason why, Harper. He's a cold-blooded killer."

We're all cold out here.

"—he's insane. He's got some secret vendetta programmed into him from years ago and he's acting it out. He failed his last psych evaluation. After he killed his brother, he failed his psych exam. They had a hit out on him—"

"What?"

"Yeah. They had a hit out on him, but the assassin got cold feet. If she had done her job—"

She?

"—we wouldn't all be so fucking paranoid right now."

"The Company has a female assassin?"

Vincent laughs. "That's your question? After what I just told you? That's your question?"

"Who is this assassin?"

"Me," a soft voice replies from the now open bedroom door. A young woman, probably the same age as me, walks into the room. Her hair is dark and long and her eyes are a brilliant green. "I'm the assassin sent to kill James."

"And who are you?" I ask, my irritation clear.

"Vincent's sister."

I look at Vincent. "She's James' missing sister? The one he thinks was kidnapped?"

Vincent sighs, his head shaking slightly. Like he's tried of explaining things to me. Or maybe more accurately, tired of having to explain the things James has been telling me. "Harper, may I introduce my sister, Nicola. This is Harper Tate."

"Pleased," she says in a snooty way that makes me want to punch her in the face. "Tet knows where I am. Or rather, where I was. I met him several times growing up. We spent a few holidays together after I was… sent away. And I spent my first six years as his sister instead of Vincent's. But unfortunately, Tet's memory—" She replaces her words with a look of sadness and a slight shake of her head. "His memory is so muddled these days, he has no idea what's up or down."

She's lying. I can feel it. I stand up and walk over to the window. It's a beautiful day out and now that it's light, I can see the Pacific Ocean. There's a community of neighboring homes surrounding the woods that line this property. Mansions, just not as big as this one. I can see the anchored boats from this window too. They call to me in a way I haven't felt in a long time. I love this view. "I don't believe you."

"What's not to believe? He lives from moment to moment." Nicola stands next to me now. She's silent and quick. As most assassins are, I'm sure. "I mean, which part are you having problems with? Maybe I can clear things up."

James' words in the desert after he fucked me in the bathroom come to mind. *I just never know which moments will count, so I treat them all the same.*

That sounds like James.

"I loved him too, Harper Tate. I loved him very much. He was a good brother when I was small. He taught me how to ride a bike. And swim. And tell time. I used to call him Tock-Tock—"

That message on the phone back in the desert. *Tock-Tock*. The message sent to the phone I found in James' little green house. Tock-Tock. It was her. Nicola. She sent that message.

We'll talk soon. Don't forget why this is happening.

What's happening? Obviously Nicola was not Sasha's kidnapper, because I killed that guy when I twisted his neck. But Nicola sent that person because she sent that message.

"—you know, Harper, that all of this is true. You know deep down that what we're saying is true."

She's right. None of what they are saying is surprising. Is he insane? Maybe. Probably a little, at least. He's done some horrific things. And I really don't have any problem imagining him doing the things they say he's done.

Except when it comes to me.

Am I delusional? Am I in that fairyland where women delude themselves into believing their captor is the good guy? What do they call that again? Stockholm Syndrome. Do I have that? Did James abduct me without knowing and then brainwash me with sex so I'd be compliant?

That was the very first thing he did. He kissed me. Under the pier. Like he was *claiming* me. Hell, he might even have used that word a time or two.

I turn and walk quickly over to the bed and sit down before I pass out.

"Nicola," Vincent says. "Can you please leave us alone for a while?"

I look up to see a sympathetic look on her face as she faces her brother, and then she gives him a nod and walks out.

"Harper." Vincent sounds tired. I wonder if he got any sleep at all last night. "I'm sorry. OK? For what it's worth, I'm sorry you have to hear this. I know you think you love him, but he's been using you. From the moment he saw you on that beach, he was plotting. Ask yourself, Harper. Why did he take you back to your father if he loves you and wanted to keep you? Why?"

I don't think that's a real question, so I say nothing.

"He took you back because the Admiral hired him to do that. You're a job to him. The Admiral wanted you left alone at the beach. Everyone knew where you were, Harper. How stupid do you think we are? But the standing order was to watch and not approach. And then Tet went crazy and killed Cy—"

"Who's Cy?"

"Tony, I mean. Our brother, Tony. Number Five. We all have nicknames that relate to a method of killing. Tony was Cy for cyanide. That's his calling card if he needs to kill people on the fly. Like, not authorized. He poisons them with cyanide."

Sick. And James said his poison was something with tet in in. Tetro something. Pufferfish poison. "Wait. You said you're not an assassin."

"I'm not."

"But you said *we* all have nicknames. And I asked you what your code was and you acted like I was stupid."

He raises his hands. "I lied, OK? We're not allowed to talk about it. Not even to you."

"So you are an assassin?"

"No. I told you, I'm the control."

"So Control is your code name?"

"I can't say, Harper. I can't say."

"So do you know that my code is?"

"You don't have a code. You're a girl."

"Nicola is a girl too, and she obviously has a code. What's her number?"

"Two. She's Number Two."

"So if she's a girl, and she's an assassin, and she has a code, then why don't you think I have a code?"

He eyes me sadly. It makes my heart skip, this look. It says so much without words, I have to gulp down some air before I forget to breathe. "Because if you do have a code, Harper, then you're part of the game too. And that means we're all in a lot more danger than I originally thought."

TWENTY

Harper

I stay in my room all day thinking about what Vincent said. Is it really true girls don't have codes? I have to be honest, I've never thought about it before. I've always had a code. It's not something Nick and I made up. My father told me. He warned me about divulging names. He said the code is the most meaningful thing about me. Which is just—what the fuck? Who says something like that to a little kid?

I was never to tell anyone. Of course, I told Nick. And he told me his. But he's been an assassin all his life. He was Eleven. That was always him. We used to joke that someday he'd knock off the first digit and just be One. He always wanted to be One.

And I was Come.

James is Six. And Tet.

Sasha was... she never told me. Hmmm. Maybe she didn't have a code then? Maybe it's true and girls don't have codes.

Come.

Come here. Come back. Come to me. Coming. There's a lot of ways to give that word meaning. But just Come? I dunno. I don't get it.

Come… it has to mean something.

A knock at the door pulls me from my thoughts. "Come in," I say and then shake my head. See? It's got a lot of possibilities.

"Sorry," Vincent says. "I'm just going down to the beach and wanted to see if you'd like to join me."

"The beach. Ummm…" It's very hard to say no to the beach. And I've been cooped up in this guest room all day. Vincent is a man of his word. He had someone fix me a room down the hall. My new clothes are even hanging in the closet. I did see the servants this time, but they were not friendly. In fact, I don't think any of them speak English. "Sure."

His face lights up at my decision. "Great. I'll pack us some food so we can eat dinner down there. Come downstairs when you're ready."

I smile as he leaves. *Come* downstairs.

The word itself implies movement towards something. Or… perhaps back to something. I shake my head and get up to find a bathing suit in my closet, putting it out of my mind. From what I know, the codes don't have meaning specifically. It's only the form of the word that counts. Verb. You're nobody. Noun, you're a little more than nobody. Ranks, you're somebody. And numbers mean you're a cold-blooded killer.

James.

Nick.

And that makes me pause as I rummage through drawers looking for a one-piece so I don't feel too exposed in front of Vincent. How is Nick any different than James?

He's not. Except he's my brother. My twin.

But… I look over at the door. Vincent is James' twin. And clearly they are not on the same side. And I don't think it's really about who gets *me*. I'm not so full of myself to make this all about me.

I think they were born for different reasons.

Just like Nick and I.

I was born to be a bargaining chip. To make allies for the Company. Like a princess in Old World Europe. To cement relationships. Which is why I never completely bought the fact that James was my promise. It never made sense. But Vincent? That does make sense. He's the kind of man my father would want me to marry. He's rich, and refined, and he seems to live in the real world as opposed to the secret one James lives in.

I guess we have something in common after all.

I change into my one-piece suit and pull a tank top and shorts over it, then slip my feet into some sandals. When I make my way downstairs I find Vincent outside drinking a beer and reading a newspaper. "Ready?" he asks, folding his paper and setting it down.

"My code is Come. I need to know yours."

He stares at me for a moment. We're not supposed to talk about this stuff but I don't care.

"Harper," he says, shaking his head. "You know I can't tell you that. And you should not have told me yours."

"What's it mean? Come? I know they're not supposed to have much meaning. But I feel like it does. What's it mean?" I ask this in a rhetorical way. Almost thinking out loud. So when Vincent opens his mouth, I'm a little taken aback.

"It's the call to action that should've happened on your eighteenth birthday."

"What?" I just stare at him like an idiot.

"Come. It's a directive, right? Come see my daughter. Come see her contribute to the society. Come see me put my allegiance above my family. Come see my sacrifice."

"You made that up."

He shrugs as he stands. "Some of it. I don't recall the exact words on the invitation."

"What?" I have to put a hand to my heart.

Vincent crosses the few steps between us and takes my hand. "The party invitation last year. It was on the directive. I mean, I had no idea it was your code, so take this for what it's worth. But I did receive an invitation that night. But I was told to wait until the next day. Good thing, huh?" He laughs. "I'd be dead right now if I had gone."

And then my words flash back to me. When I told James if I had known he was my promise I'd have done it all differently. Not killed anyone.

I look up at Vincent and wonder… would I have been so

desperate to leave if I had seen him that day? If I had known I'd be leaving that night with him, going back to his home, or yacht, or wherever? "I would not have gone through with it if I saw you there, Vincent."

"No?" He smiles big and takes my hand. "That's good to know."

And then we walk in silence down the path that leads to the beach.

But I can't help thinking about what James said. That my father used me to kill all those important people that day. That Nick gave me that Visine idea to kill them, and yet my father never drank the water.

James said Nick warned him.

And I thought that was absurd, since the Admiral was our enemy at the time. We were trying to get away from him.

Weren't we?

I'm still thinking about this when we make it to the stairs that lead down to the beach.

I scan the horizon, but it's obscured on both sides by the cliffs. It's like we're inside a little cove that shelters this beach and the marina from the strong current of the Pacific a quarter mile out. "Where's your yacht?"

"Anchored just out of sight that way," he replies, pointing south. "This marina is only for small boats."

"Oh. Maybe we can take the tender out there and hang out?"

"Not today, darling. We'll have to settle for a picnic on the beach, if that's OK."

Darling? I frown. We continue down the stairs until we finally reach the sand.

I take my sandals off immediately and strip off my clothes, the wild girl of my younger years taking over as I relish the sand between my toes. When I look up at Vincent, he's smiling.

"I've heard the rumors."

"What rumors?" I ask, dropping to the ground and stretching my legs out in the late day sun.

"About your wild nature on the beach."

I chuckle at that characterization as Vincent takes off his shirt.

Holy God. I can't stop staring at him. He's exactly like James in the muscular chest department. He catches me staring but I don't look away and neither does he. "I'm not bad, eh? You're not so hard to look at yourself. But"—he eyes my body in the one-piece suit—"I'd rather you wore the bikinis when we're on our private beach."

"*Our* beach?" I smirk at him. "You're getting ahead of yourself, don't you think?"

And then he's on top of me, forcing my body back into the hot sand, his chest pushing against my breasts, his mouth dipping closer and closer to mine as each second passes. "This is your beach, Harper. This is your home. I am your future, not James. And all you'd need to see this is to allow me one night. Tonight. Just give me one night to show you I'm the perfect man for you."

I can only stare at him. He's not pressing down hard enough to affect my breathing, but he's affecting my breathing all the same. "I can't," I finally manage.

"You can," he whispers back. His legs part so he can straddle my thighs. "You can, Harper. All you have to do is give me permission."

"Permission for what?"

"To kiss you for one."

"You've already kissed me."

"I stole those. The next one needs to be a gift. Because I want to kiss you like I mean it. And I can't steal one of those. I don't want it to be a surprise or something that catches you off guard. I want it to be purposeful, and welcomed, and returned." We stare at each other for a few more seconds and then he rolls off me and sits up and stretches his legs out on the hot sand now. He leans back on his arms and looks up at the sky. "Take your time, though. I can wait."

And then he jumps up to his feet and runs down the beach and dives into the waves. I sit up so I can see him. So I can watch that beautifully athletic body as he dips under a wave and disappears.

He is so much like James. He's nicer than James, in fact. He's patient and he wants permission.

James took. He took me the way he wanted and never asked me anything. He just assumed I was his because… because he thought my father gave me away to him as a little girl.

Vincent pops up out of the waves and starts swimming out to sea. He's a strong swimmer, I decide. He's strong because open sea swimming is not something everyone can do and James does it—

Wait. Not James. *Vincent.* Vincent does it effortlessly. Good God, I'm starting to mix them up.

I watch him swim and when he comes back there is no more mention of kissing. We eat the picnic food he packed and watch the sun set on the ocean. Vincent chats through it and thinking back on it now, sitting in bed trying to remember the things that make me belong to James and not Vincent, that's one of them.

The sunsets.

James owns my sunsets.

TWENTY-ONE

Harper

I go to the beach alone the next day. Vincent is busy with… whatever. I'm not really sure what he does, but he left a note on the bedside table saying he would not be around and I should feel free to amuse myself today.

No restrictions. No guidelines. No rules.

Weird.

So I'm at the marina staring out at the sea. There's a boat way out there, but from experience, I know what it is. A megayacht. I can tell by the top side that there's a helipad, so I'm guessing that's the yacht we came in on.

I look over at the boats docked in neat little rows. There are not a lot of them, it's a small marina. Before I know it, I'm on my feet walking. The dock is metal and my feet pound as I walk the length of it looking at each boat. I know what a tender looks like. I mean, they come in all shapes and sizes, but I do remember what the tender looked like that we took from my father's yacht to Vincent's. It was large. One that held a lot of people. And it had a cabin for the helmsman.

My eyes scan the available boats until they rest on one at the end of the dock. I walk up to it and read the name. *Illegal Tender*. Cute. But very telling. It's a tender boat all right. And that means it belongs to the yacht anchored offshore. I step inside and take it in. My eyes immediately go to the control panel. To the ignition. To the lockbox built into the side of the boat. I open it and there's the key. Or at least, one key. That's where we keep our keys when we're docked somewhere private. So I guess whoever this person is out on that ship has something in common with my own family.

Besides me, of course.

I look back at the beach and then up to the tip of the mansion's roof that is just barely visible from this low angle. I sit in the helmsman's chair and start the boat.

She purrs.

I smile.

God, I have missed the water. The beach is not the same. I jump up, untie the boat, and then take my seat and ease her away from the dock. The Pacific is strong and the waves are looming, but I'm not in a rush. So I take it slow. Just casually meander my way towards the yacht. It takes a good while for me to get close enough to see her name—*Barely Legal*, another very telling sign that these are Company people—and then a few minutes later I can see a crew member waiting for me in the garage.

Megayachts always have a tender boat. It's a limousine used to shuttle passengers to the shore. Our yachts actually have two, but the sailing ship, the one I escaped from last year, only had one. A quick look inside the garage tells me this one has space for two, but none are here at the moment.

The crewman says nothing to me as he secures the vessel, and I ignore him as well. I've grown up around servants and I learned to ignore most of them very early. Not because I was snooty, just because it was a rule. I was not allowed to talk to people, status in life notwithstanding, and that was something I took very seriously. James didn't even know my name until I told him that morning under the pier. He asked me on the beach back when we become Six, but I kept that secret like I was supposed to.

Actually—my mind wanders as I make my way through the garage and towards the entrance into the main part of the ship—

Nick saw me drawing pictures in the sand. I was trying to give James a hint so I drew all the instruments I could remember from an orchestra. The last one was a harp and I had been hoping he would guess my name when he looked down at it.

But Nick came, calling me *sister*, which meant he was mad. And then he ushered me away from James and back to the ship.

Where I proceeded to spend the day not with James, as I had thought, but with Vincent.

I could not tell the difference.

Of course, I was six.

I open the hatch and walk into the ship. There's a ladder so I climb, because I know full well I'm not going to find the owner of this boat down here. The next floor up also has a ladder, so I climb again. This floor has decks. But not the deck I'm looking for. So I go up one more level. This is a big-ass ship.

I hear soft music playing in the saloon area and when I step in, the cramped companionway opens up to a room filled with sleek, modern furniture.

"There she is," a woman's voice says from off to my left. She's middle age, maybe mid-fifties. Her hair is dark and piled high on her head in an extravagant updo that contrasts with her beachwear. She tips her sunglasses down her nose and stares at me with brilliant green eyes.

So they get them from their mother, I catch myself thinking as she stands and extends her hand, walking towards me. "Harper Tate," she coos as she waits for me to shake her hand. I do that, I'm on autopilot, and her grip is soft and so are her hands. "Finally, we get to see the golden child."

I step back. "I'm sorry," I say politely. "I'm at a disadvantage here."

"Oh," the mother coos again. "Albert, I do believe your son has neglected his manners." She looks over my shoulder and I turn to greet Albert.

I'm so glad my back is to the mother, because Albert is a drooling old man in a wheelchair. His head lies against his shoulder and his hands are secured to the arms of his wheelchair with Velcro strips.

He's wearing a bib.

This. Is James' father.

The *titular* head of a Company family. And from what my father said, only this family competes with our rank. Company royalty, he called my future children.

I look back to the mother and take her in again, this time seeing her for what she really is. The *actual* head of a global shadow government. A woman who not only bargains the lives of girls but sends sons off to kill on command.

"Mrs. Albert Fenici," she says as she watches me. "Now tell me, dear, what can I do for you?" If my stunned silence bothers her, she keeps that tucked away. "Oh, come now, Harper. Relax. We're practically family now. I've been told you're a nervous girl. Have a drink with me and settle down on the couch over there." She points and I wander over there automatically.

I don't know why I'm so off guard. I'm just… surprised to learn the person in charge of all these atrocities is a woman.

"How is Vincent treating you, dear? Well?" I don't answer. "And how is your father? I haven't seen him in ages." She smiles and allows herself a small laugh as she drops ice cubes into a tumbler from behind the bar. "What's your poison?"

"Huh?" I ask back, coming out of my stupor.

"Your drink, dear. What do you like to drink?"

"Bottled water, please."

She laughs again and pours me something from a bottle all right. But it's not water. "Try this." She walks over to me, her gauzy robe flaring out behind her and her strappy stiletto sandals clicking on the hardwood deck. My nanny was wrong after all. Stilettos are perfectly acceptable footwear on a ship.

I put a hand up as she tries to give me the drink. "I can't, I'm sorry. I took an Ativan today and I shouldn't drink when I take the pills."

"Oh." She looks at me in a new way. She—studies me. As if she's trying to detect the effects of the drug. But after a few seconds she takes the drink back to the bar and sets it on the stone counter.

I guess whatever she poured me is not her poison of choice.

"Are you not a talker, darling?"

"How?" is all that comes out.

"How what?" She blinks at me.

I consider my choices right now. "How do you live with yourself knowing you sent him off to kill?"

I could play her game.

Her smile drops and her jaw clenches. "James, you mean? Or Tony? Or perhaps you mean my daughter, Nicola?"

Or I could humor her.

"All of the above."

"It's Company policy, darling. You will send your children off as well. Soon," she says, pointing her glass at my belly.

Or I could kill her.

"I could snap your neck right now."

"What?"

"Just twist it, like I did that assassin on the dirt bike who tried to take Sasha."

"You do know what side you're on? *Whose* side you're on?"

The familiar *womp-womp-womp* of a helicopter invades the conversation as it makes an approach.

"I could get even for what you made him do. I could—"

I say more and more, but the helicopter is so loud now it steals my words. But I look at her face and that's all I need. I will remember the horror she feels in this moment when she realizes she underestimated me. When she realizes one half-dead man in a wheelchair can't save her if I decide to end her reign of terror.

The ship rocks as the bird lands and she spills her drink because those fucking shoes really aren't appropriate footwear for a boat and they make her stumble.

"Harper," Vincent yells over the thumping blades as he grips the sides of the ladder and jumps down to our deck. He crosses the room and stands between me and his mother. His hair is a mess. In fact, he's sort of a mess all over. His shirt is open at the top and he's got no jacket and no tie on. Like he just rolled out of bed.

Asshole. He probably has a girl in that house who will fuck him. He probably spent the day with her.

"Let's go," he says, leaning way down into my ear. His grip on my hand never softens. It's rigid and tight. He places a hand on my other elbow, guiding me past his mother as we make our way to the ladder that will take us to the heliport.

Her hand snaps out as I pass her and the ice-cold contents of her glass splash all over my face.

"Stop it," Vincent yells, pushing her back when she comes at me.

"How dare that little whore say such things to me."

I wiggle in Vincent's tight grip and manage to turn around enough to snarl at her. "Bitch. You're a bitch who deserves to die for what you did. I will kill you! I will fucking kill you!"

Vincent actually picks me up and carries me over to the ladder, then places my feet on the third rung and orders me to climb.

I climb. But my heart is beating fast. And I realize, as I'm ushered into the helicopter like we're in a war zone, it's not from fear.

It's from hate.

This is what it feels like to hate.

TWENTY-TWO

Harper

The ride back to the house only takes a few minutes. We don't even bother to put our headsets. And from the look on Vincent's face, he's not in the mood to talk.

I'm not either.

When the helicopter lands Vincent pushes me to scoot out, and then he follows me. He puts his arms around my shoulders and walks me out from under the rotating blades.

We don't talk. We just walk all the way to the house and I wait for him to open the door and allow me to pass through.

"Would you like to tell me what that was all about?" he asks, once we're both inside the house.

I don't want to think about it. "I'm tired."

"Too bad."

I look up at him with a sneer. "Yeah, too bad for you if you want to know. Because I'm not interested in talking."

His jaw clenches but instead of continuing the fight, he takes my hand and leads me down the hallway towards the kitchen.

"What are you doing?"

"Eating dinner." We stop at the entrance to the kitchen and he feels around for the light switch. After the darkness of the house, it's blinding. I bow my head and close my eyes, too worn out from that confrontation to care about food.

"Sit, Harper. I'll make us something."

I walk over to the stainless-steel island and sit on a stainless-steel stool as Vincent rummages around the kitchen looking for things. My legs are so cold from the metal chair I begin to shiver. "I'm not hungry, Vincent. I just want to go to bed."

"You'll be in bed soon enough. But first we're going to eat." He stares at the assortment of things he's collected on the counter and then goes looking for something else. "Tell me something, Harper."

"What?" I scowl at his back. "I don't feel like talking about it, OK? You're not going to like the answer anyway."

"Forget about my bitch of a mother," he says, dragging a waffle iron out of a cupboard. "Tell me why I'm not good enough for you." He starts measuring flour and pouring it into a bowl. And as he does that I study him from behind. His back is well-defined. I can see his muscles working through his white dress shirt. He stops what he's doing and rolls up his sleeves, then proceeds with his preparation. "I look like him. I sound like him." His voice lowers for that. A deep rumble that makes me swallow. Because he does look and sound an awful lot like James. "I'm sure the fuck nicer than him." And then he stops what he's doing and looks over his shoulder. "You'd have to agree on that."

I shrug. "James is very nice too."

"He's insane. They all say he's insane. He went off that first year to do his killing and he came back damaged behind repair."

"Do you know what happened?" I bite my lip, not really sure if I want to know or not.

"Everyone knows what happened."

"Everyone but me."

He's silent as he mixes up the batter, his motions unhurried and deliberate. Like he's made a lot of waffles in his life and he knows just what to do. There's no recipe either. He just threw some things in a bowl.

"Will you tell me?"

"Do you really want to know?" He looks over his shoulder

again. "I *should* tell you. Then maybe you'll change your mind about him and settle for this life instead."

"Do you want me if I have to settle?"

"I want you any way I can get you." He finishes his mixing and sets the bowl aside before turning around to face me. "But it's not fair to take you. It's not fair to you, and it's not fair to me, and it's not fair to our future children."

God. He's handsome. I can't deny it. He's so much like James. "I don't think it would change my mind if I knew what happened to him. I think it would make me love him more."

"Huh," Vincent says as he crosses his arms in front of his chest. "I doubt that."

"Tell me, then. Maybe this is your chance to win me over."

He stares hard at me. His gaze is like steel. Cold and hard. He doesn't look like the man who's been trying to win me these past few days. He looks like I've pushed him past his breaking point. Like this confrontation with his mother was the last straw. "Twelve years ago James Fenici went on a mission to Central America and never came back."

"He came back. He just came back later than expected."

But Vincent shakes his head. "No. James never came back. Tet came back."

"He's not two people, Vincent. He's just James."

"He's not two people, you're right. He's just Tet. James died in that Honduran prison. They starved him. Deprived him of water. Of basic facilities. They locked him in a cell that was not long enough to stretch out and not tall enough to stand up. And when it became clear that the Company wasn't going to negotiate to get him back, even though he was the son of one of the most powerful elite members, they made him a slave and tortured him."

I'm stuck on the word *slave*.

"But we all get mentors when we come of age. And James got One as his mentor. One. The same man who tried to kill you last week is the man who saved James that first year. It was a large debt to owe. Do you understand that?"

I never stop looking at Vincent. I can't take my eyes off him. His arm muscles are contracting even as he tries to keep them steady across his chest. His jaw is clenching again. His hands are squeezed together into fists. "I don't understand it, Vincent. I don't know what that means to have a large debt."

"Neither did James."

Vincent turns around and starts pouring batter into the waffle iron. I watch him work and then when he's done, he closes the lid and pushes a button before turning back to me. He looks slightly calmer than he did, but he's still very tense.

"It means he owed One his life. He owed One his loyalty. He owed One everything. So every time One came to him with a request, James had to say yes."

My heart is beating faster now. "What did he say yes to?"

"Vengeance murders. Drug dealing. Torture. And..." The waffle iron beeps and he turns to flip it over.

"And what else?"

"And... he kept secrets. Secrets One had. Secrets that need to be told."

I wait for Vincent to elaborate, but he keeps his back to me. "That's not enough," I tell his back. "That's not enough to change my mind about him."

"That's because you have no details, Miss Tate." He turns his attention back to me. "The details are what change the hearts and minds."

"He told me he killed hundreds of people. He told me all this. But I'm a killer too. You know that. I'm not innocent. I keep secrets. I have lots of secrets. Secrets about very bad men."

"James Fenici is the worst of all those very bad men, Harper. The worst."

"What secrets then? If the devil's in the details, then give me details."

Vincent lifts the waffles out of the waffle iron with a fork and plops them down on a plate. The delicious smell is in stark contrast to the conversation we're having. It feels surreal. He spreads some butter over the little checkered pattern in the pastry, then dribbles maple syrup on top. His fingertips reach into a bag of powdered sugar and he flicks that over the syrup until it's coated in white specks.

He walks the plate over to me and sets it down on the metal counter with a ting that rings through the room. "Fork?" he asks, holding one out for me.

"Thank you." I take the fork and cut a little piece of waffle off as he leans over the counter and watches. I bring it to my mouth and for some reason, eating in front of him stirs me. My sex throbs for a moment as I take in the food and realize his gaze is trained on me. Only me. "Aren't you going to eat?"

The smile wipes away the tense conversation and his eyes light up a bit. "Feed me." And then he sends me a wicked grin that makes the throbbing grow.

I cut off another piece of waffle and bring it to his lips. "Tell me what secrets James kept."

He opens his mouth and I place the food on his tongue, unable to stop watching his lips as they close around the fork. I pull it away and have to remind myself to breathe.

He points to the plate. "How about I feed you? You eat, and I'll talk."

I'm surprised it's so easy to get the answers I'm looking for, but I'm in no position to argue, so I nod and hand him the fork.

He cuts off a piece of waffle and brings it to my mouth. I open for him, but at the last second he leans in and kisses me. He tastes like syrup and pastry. He tastes like breakfast with someone you love. He tastes like the life I wish I had. A normal life with no secrets. I've never wanted secrets. I've never wanted to know them. All my life I've been running from the facts, and now here I am, begging for them.

"You have to kiss me after every secret," he whispers into my mouth. "You have to kiss me when I tell you these things or I won't be able to do it." And then he pulls back and brings the fork forward. I open my mouth for the food and he places it on my tongue until I grab it with my teeth and begin to chew.

"Say yes to that, Harper Tate, and I'll tell you everything you think you want to know for the price of a kiss."

I nod. I know the kiss is wrong, but it doesn't feel wrong right now. It feels right in every way imaginable. "OK," I whisper back.

"Nicola was given away when she was six. And James was the one who gave her away." Vincent watches me for a reaction, but all I can do is stare into his eyes. "One knew he was never going to get a promise, so he asked James to give him his sister."

"But… he told me that his mother and father gave her away. He told me—"

"He lied." It cuts me off, that's how forceful the declaration is. "He lies a lot, Harper. Even to you. Especially to you. He lies to himself too. The notebook was a lie, Harper. A delusional, fake world he talked himself into believing... because he couldn't cope with the truth."

The last few words come out soft. Almost a whisper. "What's the truth, Vincent."

He stares at me. Perhaps considering if this is a time to tell the truth or lie. But then he lets out a breath and I know what's coming is the truth. "The truth that he got what he asked for. He chose that life and he got everything that came with it."

"And his sister? What's the truth about her?"

"James gave his sister away to One to pay his debt. That's secret number one and now I get a kiss." Vincent leans in and brushes his lips against mine. Softly. Like his words. Tenderly. Like his touch. It's not demanding and harsh. It's almost begging for forgiveness. "You don't want James. You want Vincent."

I push him back and shake my head. "He must've known she'd be taken care of, though. That One would take care of her."

Vincent tries to smile and fails, so he cuts off another piece of waffle and feeds it to me instead. I chew slowly, trying to figure out what it is we're doing here.

"Do you want more?"

"Yes," I say. "If there's more, I should know."

He tips his chin up a little like that stung him. I'm sure he was counting on that driving a wedge between me and my love for James, but it can't be the whole story. There has to be more.

"I need to hear it all," I say. "If it's all been a lie, then I need the truth. I can't make decisions based on lies."

"I know that," he says, looking back down at the food. "That's why I'm here."

"So tell me the rest."

"One trained her to fight. He trained her to kill. He trained her to lie, and steal, and cheat. He turned her into one of us. But before any of that could happen, the little girl needed to be comforted. She was ripped from her home. She was ripped from her family.

She did nothing but cry for weeks. For months. And James was the one who settled her down."

"How?" I picture this lost little girl, crying for her family. Locked away somewhere dark and scary.

"He told her lies, Harper. He lied to her for years and years. He told her how she would go home one day and see her family. He told her she'd live like a princess if she obeyed. He told her everything her little girl heart wanted to hear."

"How old was James when he did this?"

Vincent shrugs as he presumably counts back the years. "It started at sixteen and went on until he was eighteen or nineteen, at least."

"And that Nicola I met the other day? She's the one?"

Vincent stares at me but says nothing.

"Because she looked fine to me. She sounded like a snooty rich girl, in fact. You said she's an assassin. Good for her, I guess. So is Nick. So is James. It's just a job, Vincent. Isn't that what they always tell us? Everyone in the Company has a job. I have a job. I have to marry you and have babies. Did you ever ask me if I wanted to have babies? What if I don't want to run board meetings? What if I'd rather be a marine biologist? Or a dog trainer? Maybe I'd rather be anything but this fucking girl sitting in this stupid industrial kitchen. Maybe Nicola has a better life as an assassin. Did you ever ask her? Maybe James did the right thing, getting her away from that wicked mother. Did that ever occur to you?"

I stare at him and he smiles as he leans in for a kiss. "You really are a lionfish, you know that?" And then his tongue slips in and his hand slides around my neck to keep me from pulling back. I open my mouth to him, responding to his request, and he moans and wraps his arms all the way around me. He scoots the stool closer to him, one hand sliding under to grab my ass, the other clasping me firmly by the neck. "I want you so fucking bad. I want to flip you over and fuck you right now."

I squirm away and place a hand on his chest, but he grabs my wrists and yanks them behind my back. "That was a secret, so I get a kiss." I turn my head when he tries and then he lets go and steps back. "You're cheating."

"You're cheating," I say back. "That wasn't a secret. I want another one. Maybe I'm just a cold-hearted bitch, but boo fucking hoo for your sister. She doesn't look so bad. I mean, I was trained by my brother too. What's the difference? I was given to you. What's the difference? So she got different parents? From what I can tell, that bitch of a mother of yours does not deserve children."

He's shaking his head the whole time I'm talking and so when I stop, I expect a protest. But he gives me silence instead. He looks away, then back, then away again. "One beat her," he finally admits.

I swallow down *that* bitter truth. "Well, I'm sorry for that, of course. I'm sorry for that. No one deserves to get beaten. But One strangled me unconscious last week. I was drugged. Overdosed, in fact. So it looks like One does not discriminate when it comes to who he wants to abuse. And if the guy is one of the oldest, more seasoned assassins, then that means if he wanted your sister, he would have her. With or without help from James." I stop talking and just stare at him. "Next."

Vincent breaks a smile at that response. "You want more kisses, don't you?"

I laugh under my breath. "No, I just want to know more about James. I want to know everything about James."

"It's all bad stuff, Harper. Why would you want to know? Why him? When I'm right here? Why bother with damaged when you can have perfect?"

"No one's perfect, Vincent. You can't tell me you grew up in this fucked-up family and came out perfect. It doesn't matter how nice things look on the outside, it's a lie. And we both know it."

"He drowned our father. He tried to kill our father, but he failed."

Now that has my attention.

Vincent nods. "He is the one who drowned him, Harper. James held him under the water for so long he came back to life brain-damaged—"

"I don't care."

Vincent looks at me and shakes his head. "What the fuck is wrong with you?"

"I don't care."

"He stalked you, Harper. He lied to you about being your promise. He knew the Admiral took that offer back. He stalked you all growing up. He's dangerous and one day he's gonna get you killed."

"I don't care."

"He's evil, Harper. He's got no soul. He's got no conscience—"

"*I don't care.*"

Vincent reaches out and snatches my hand. I gasp from the sudden movement, and then again when I realize he's placed it over his hard cock. "James used you to get this party. He's using you to get revenge. You know what Come means? Come get me. Come here. Come find me. It's a calling card to bring people together so they can be killed. You're the fucking bait! Just like James was born to kill, you were born to be bait. So your father can kill. So my mother can kill. And he knows that. He set you up."

"I don't care, I said. I don't fucking care."

His hand squeezes mine, making me grip him. Or maybe I just *want* to grip him. His cock is just as big as James'. And when I look up, his eyes, his hair, his body—all of it says James to me.

He's lifting my shirt off over my head before I even realize he's not forcing me to cup his dick anymore. Yet I still hold it firm in my grasp. He flicks a nipple and then his mouth covers it, biting and twisting.

"Fuck," he says as he brings his mouth to my neck. "I'm gonna fuck you unless you put up a fight. You understand? I can't stand it anymore. I can't wait any longer."

I fully intend to pull back and put a stop to this, but then he slaps my tit, making it sting and bounce against my flesh. I'm shocked. Too shocked to even react, and then he does it again. He grabs my chin and holds it just a little bit too tight. Just enough to make the wetness that's been building between my legs explode. "Oh, God," I moan.

"James likes it rough, Harper. Do you want it rough? Vincent will fuck you nicely."

"I want it rough. I like it rough," I call out. "I want it hard. I want it so fucking hard."

He scoops me up in his arms and carries me out of the kitchen.

TWENTY-THREE

Harper

He sets me down in the hallway and backs me up against the wall. "Fuck," he says, pausing to take a deep breath. "I need to know if this is what you want, Harper. I can't go on unless I know you want to fuck me as bad as I want to fuck you."

His head is bowed and his hair falls forward, obscuring his eyes. His chest is rising and falling rapidly, like his heart is beating as fast as mine.

I don't know what to say. I don't want him, I want James. But he's all I have right now.

"Just tell me," he says urgently. "Just tell me what you're thinking. Right now."

"You're not going to like it."

He bumps his forehead to mine, still looking down at the floor. "Just say it. I need to hear the truth."

I'm so horny. My fingers dip between my legs and I start rubbing myself in small circles. If I could just get this release, I could think clearly again. I know it. If I could—

Vincent removes my hand and brings my fingers to his mouth.

He looks me in the eye as he sucks on them, then kisses the tips and places my hand over his heart. "Feel me. Can you feel me? I need to know what you're thinking. I need to know once and for all if you'll be mine." And then he takes my hand and places it over my heart. I feel the same staccato rhythm as his.

This is too much, my heart says. But I can't lie. "I'm in love with James, Vincent. I am. I'm sorry. I know you look like him and Jesus, you act so much like him sometimes. But you're not him."

He stares at me for a moment and then he turns me around and hugs my body tightly to his. "But you need to get off? You need the release? Because I'll do that for you, Harper. I'll take away all this tension so you can think straight again."

Before I can answer, one hand slips between my folds and begins to rub while the other one grabs my breast fiercely. So hard I moan from the pain. He lets go and slaps it again. And when his finger slides inside me, I'm so wet I can barely feel him. "More," I moan. "More."

Two more fingers enter my pussy and he dips his mouth down to my neck and whispers in my ear as he plays me like an instrument. "You're so pretty. You're so pretty, Harper. I want to fuck your pretty pussy so bad right now, you have no idea. I want to stuff my cock in your ass and make you squeeze it when you come."

Holy fuck. "I'm gonna come right now."

He bites me on the shoulder and that's all I need to push me over the edge. The pain of his mouth. The pleasure of his fingers. The hard bulge pushing up against my ass as he forces my face into the wall.

"Come," he commands. "Come right now, Harper."

I couldn't stop it if I tried. I'm gone. I'm blown. My self-control is over. My back buckles as his whole hand slaps against my pussy. I come, and come again. Wave after wave of trembling pleasure spills out of me. By the time I'm done, I can no longer stand and I drop to my knees.

Vincent's hands are on my head, urging me to turn around. I plop down on my butt and turn to face him, my back pressing up against the hallway wall. I look up in his eyes and then my gaze goes to his hand on his cock. The bulge underneath his trousers is huge. It's hard. And his face looks like he needs a release.

But he doesn't ask me. He just waits.

My hands go to his belt and I unbuckle it, letting the slack sides fall down his thighs. I unbutton him, and then drag the zipper down. I reach inside and pull his cock out.

It's so big. Just as big as I remember. "James," I say before I remember this is not James.

I expect Vincent to get angry for mixing him up, but he doesn't even notice. He just urges my mouth forward with slight pressure on my head. "Take it, Harper. Take all of it."

I open my mouth and he pushes his dick past my lips until it crashes against my soft palate, making me gag. "Breathe," he whispers. "Just breathe."

I listen. I watch him. My eyes never leave his as he begins to rock his hips forward and back. And each time his tip hits that sensitive spot that makes me want to gag, he pets my hair. "You're so pretty. You're so fucking pretty. Your pretty mouth swallowing my cock, Harper. It drives me wild."

I moan at his dirty words and this makes him throw his head back and force himself inside me even harder. "Take it, Harper. Take it."

I open wider. I flatten my tongue against his long, thick shaft. And I take all of him. He pumps a few more times and then he lets off a roar that signals his release. His dick pulses inside my mouth—once, twice, three times—and then the salty liquid is pouring down my throat.

I swallow and swallow again. And then I feel him relax and withdraw.

My eyes are closed now, but they open when he bends down so his mouth can touch mine in a soft kiss. "I'm gonna take your pretty pussy next, Harper Tate. And then that ass."

Then he stands up and tucks his dick back inside his pants.

And walks away.

TWENTY-FOUR

Harper

The next morning I wake early. When I check the clock it says five-eighteen. Did I really suck off Vincent in the hallway last night? How fucking humiliating. After he made those dirty remarks about me and James. How he said he saw us. And then he took me out of the kitchen on purpose, so he could fuck my mouth in the hall.

I'm filled with rage. And shame. And regret.

Jesus Christ. I might as well just be with him since I just fucked everything up with James. I highly doubt he's the forgiving type. Good God, for all I know he'll kill me for what I did last night.

Insane, they say.

I mean, yeah, I can certainly see it. You have to be insane to kill people like that. And the whole prisoner-of-war thing. Vincent gave me a lot of information last night. A lot of bad information about James. He wants me to hate James. At the very least, he wants me to fear James.

And I do fear James. I do. I fear that he will find out what I did last night and never want me again. I fear that he's dead somewhere. That the Company got to him and killed him before he could come back to me.

I fear that I've made a mistake that will change my life forever. A mistake that can't be undone.

And Vincent's confession about Nicola. If he's been as forthcoming with her about how she ended up as Number Two as he was with me, well, I can imagine she hates James. In fact, I can't think of a single person alive who doesn't hate James aside from me.

My heart sinks. My life feels like it's over. I hate this Company. I hate this house. I want to go back to the desert and fuck in the heat. I want the Hummer. And Sasha.

That makes me cry.

Sasha is dead. And no amount of wanting will bring her back.

And now I come full-circle, thinking James is the devil. An evil demon who kills on command. Because he shot a little girl in cold blood.

I need to get out of here.

I throw the covers off me, put my clothes back on from yesterday, and then head downstairs to the kitchen. It's still dark outside, but I can feel the dawn creeping up over the horizon when I look out the eastern windows.

There's a light on in the kitchen and the sounds of someone doing dishes.

We forgot to clean up our mess last night. We never even finished our waffle. I walk into the kitchen expecting to see the maid, and then stop dead when it's Vincent placing the dishes in the sink.

He looks at me and smiles. I can't manage one myself.

"Someone got hungry last night." He shoots me a good-natured grin and I stop in my tracks.

"What?"

"This," he says, pointing to the mess. "If I knew you were a cook, I'd have asked for something special already.'

"What?" I can't breathe.

"Are you OK, Harper?" He turns to look at me for a moment. "I'm sorry I never showed for dinner. I just didn't feel well and ended up going to bed early. But it's OK," he says, fanning his hand at the flour and eggs that were left out on the counter. "This is your home too. So help yourself if you get hungry. You don't have to wait for me to feed you."

I can't breathe.

"So what did you do last night?" He turns the water on and lets it run in the bowl that's still half full of unused batter. "Besides make a mess in the kitchen?" He smiles at me over his shoulder.

"What time did you go to bed?"

"I was so sick. It must've been the seafood I had at lunch yesterday. It's a good thing I didn't bring you along or we'd both have been sick last night."

Is he joking?

"You look tired, baby. You should go back to bed. People won't be arriving until tonight."

"What?" Oh my God, it's like I'm in an alternate universe.

"Harper," he laughs. "What's gotten into you? The party is tomorrow, baby. Nick said he'll be here tonight. That should make you happy."

"Nick is gonna be here." I do a little jump and clap my hands, the weirdness forgotten for a moment. "I can't wait!"

"That's better." And then he walks over and kisses me on the lips like we're a married couple and we meet in the kitchen every morning before he goes to work so we can talk about our upcoming day.

The weird is back. But Vincent is already walking away. "Be good, Harp."

And then I'm alone.

I walk quickly back to my room and shut the door as I try to fit the pieces of this puzzle together. Did I imagine last night? No! Surely not. The mess was right there in the kitchen.

Did he forget? Was he so sick that he forgot I sucked his dick in the hallway?

But then the bathroom door creaks as someone pushes it open. "I thought he'd never fucking leave," the deep voice rumbles and makes my whole body tingle. "I told you. I'm gonna fuck that pretty little pussy and take your ass too."

I'm too stunned to move, but the man in my room isn't. He walks towards me like he owns the entire world and stops when he's close enough to force me to look up to see him properly.

"I told you I'd come back."

James did say that.

But this isn't James. I can see the difference in his eyes.

This is Tet.

PART THREE

TWENTY-FIVE

Sasha

I don't think it's possible to bite my fingernails down any closer to the quick, but my mouth doesn't seem to notice as we pull into the Cabazon parking lot, home to Interstate 10's larger-than-life resident reptiles.

I was just here a few days ago and it seems like my life is moving in circles.

"That's them," I tell Merc. "In the red truck."

Merc mutters under his breath. "Fuck." He turns into the parking lot and two men exit the red truck and start walking to the underbelly of the brontosaurus.

"Park close, so I can hear. Like right up next to it."

Merc does not park close. Instead he drives past the two men and stares them down. Then he pulls into a spot a good hundred feet from where they are meeting.

"Merc."

"Shut up," he barks at me. "Sit your ass in this truck and do not move, do you hear me?"

"I'm the one who knows them."

"I don't give a fuck. I'm the one who's doing business. Little girls do not cut deals with international street gangs. I don't care how fucking tough you think you are, Cherlin, you're still Zero to me. So shut your mouth and do not even think about getting out."

I cross my arms over my chest and huff out some air. "It was my idea."

"Yeah, well, an idea doesn't keep you alive when you're double-dealing with scumbags like these guys. And when I tell them what we're offering, they are gonna jump on it, Smurf. So this is your last chance to call it off. Because once we have a deal, there's no turning back. People will die tomorrow. You got that?" He waits for me to answer, but I don't. I just swallow it down. "Do you understand that?" he asks again, this time grabbing my arm and squeezing tight.

"I get it, OK? But what other choice do we have? We need firepower. We need boots on the ground. We need them to kill if we want to have any chance at all of getting Harper and Nick back."

"Look, Sasha, just because you said you want Nick and Harper to get out alive doesn't mean they will. These guys know who they are. They know who their father is. They know their connections. So they might just double-cross us and kill everyone. Including you and me. Or maybe, and this is far more likely, they will take us all prisoner. And then we'll all get to experience what James went through down in Honduras twelve years ago. So I'm gonna ask you one more time. Do you really want to give James up to save your boyfriend? Because they want him, Cherlin. They want him bad."

"I told you. He's not gonna get caught. James will never get caught. They want One too, so they'll be happy to get him. James will get away, I know it. He's so much smarter. So much more lethal. If anyone can pull us through this plan, it's James."

"Not James, kid. Tet. I don't know why the fuck you can't see him for what he is. A messed-up dude with questionable loyalties."

"It doesn't matter. They're the same guy. So if Tet can do it, then James can too."

Merc draws in a long breath of air and then opens his door, leaving the truck running. "OK. Be right back." He holds out his palm and I scribble the address down on the back of a map I found in the glove box. I marked the Santa Barbara community on there as best I could on the front too. Just to make sure they get it right. Drug dealers, ya know? Not the brightest of the bunch.

Merc takes the map and pushes the door closed so it doesn't slam. Then he walks off into the sun, his shades down and his dark hair blowing a bit in the hot wind.

I hold my breath as he approaches the two men standing underneath the giant dinosaur. They don't shake hands and I see that as a bad sign. But then I see heads nodding, so that eases me a bit.

I bite my fingers again. Geez. I can't take the tension. I'm really not cut out for this hardcore dealing. I'm not. I'm just a little kid. I have no idea what I'm doing. I'm gonna get everyone killed with this idea.

But then the two men look at each other and smile. One even laughs and claps the other on the back. Merc hands them the map and they put their heads together to study it.

There's more negotiation, then they all look over at me. My stomach flips. I swear, I almost open the door and puke.

This is it. This is where Merc tells them about Nick and Harper and asks for immunity. They already have the coordinates, so they're the ones calling the shots. That was Merc's idea. Give them the upper hand and let them make this decision on their own. *That's the only way it will work,* he said. *They have to want the deal. We can't coerce them and expect co-operation.*

My leg is going a mile a minute as they hash things out. They look over at me several more times, and then there's some heated discussion.

I can only imagine what they are saying.

They want Nick. They want Harper.

And it makes sense for them, right? They want the children of the man who sent them so much trouble and strife over the years down in Central America. They want to teach him a lesson and they are ready and willing to send the LA chapter of their gang if they think they have the chance.

And I know what Merc's response will be.

You can have James. The kid who shot your leader twelve years ago. You can have his rescuer. The assassin who broke him out and mowed down the deformed man's entire family—mostly women and children—to do it.

I know this part. And no one else does besides Merc, because I told him. Probably not even James knows this part. Because this was how One got in to the compound to find James. James only knows what happened after.

I know this because One is my mother's brother. My uncle. The uncle who used to come to our house every New Year's Eve until I was ten and get drunk with my father so they could talk about my mother. Share her memory.

He used to ruffle my hair and whisper, "You have a number, Sasha. Not a name, a number. You're Zero. The one no one sees. The one no one expects. The one who will set it all right."

Of course, back then I had no idea what he was talking about. I had no idea what he was really talking about until James told me the Company had my parents killed. He told me this right here, in this parking lot. As I was sitting on the toe of a giant brontosaurus.

She needs to hear this, he told Harper.

He wanted me to know what I was up against.

Suddenly the little group of men breaks up and Merc is walking back to the truck.

My stomach flips again as I try to read his expression, but I can't, it's no use. So I hold my breath until he gets back in the truck and says, "It's done."

I exhale.

"They took the bait." He looks over at me. "Now what?"

This is the last part of the plan. The really dangerous part. The part that might get all of us killed. Because this gang might be notorious for their ruthless revenge killings, but the person I need to bring in next isn't called Number One for nothing. "Next I call my uncle."

Merc clenches his jaw, his eyes darting back and forth as he thinks this through. "You wanna know why they were laughing back there?" he asks.

No. "Yes."

"They were laughing because they said if they see James, they're not gonna kill him."

"No?" I ask, hopeful.

Merc starts the truck and backs out of the space, then heads towards the exit. "Nope." And then he looks me in the eye as he waits to turn left to get back on the Interstate. "They're gonna douse him in gasoline, set him on fire, and then put it out."

"What?"

"They're gonna make sure he lives to feel the pain."

TWENTY-SIX

Harper

"I might not've been all there this past year or so," Tet says, coming forward a few paces. "But Harper Tate, the minute I saw you on the beach, it started coming back. It took me a while, but I'm here now. I'm not the person they say I am." He turns his head and then gives me a sidelong glance. "At least not when it comes to you."

He steps forward a few more paces and I automatically put my hands up to ward him off. He grabs my wrists and hikes my hands above my head, walking me backwards until I hit the wall. I press myself flat, but he leans in and touches his lips to mine. "It would kill me, Harper Tate, if you were afraid of me."

"That was you last night."

"That was me."

"Why didn't you tell me?"

"I wanted to give you a chance to choose. A chance to choose a safer life than the one I can provide. I've got money. I've got assets. But I can't keep you safe, Harper. It would not be possible."

I just stare at him. What is he saying? "So you don't want me?

You're going to pull one of those selfish I'm-doing-this-for-your-own-good moves? Because if so, James Fenici, I'm gonna fight you over it. I swear to God, I will—"

He leans down and kisses me, laughing into my mouth. "I love you."

"I love *you*. Don't leave me. Please."

He pulls back just the slightest little bit and I look up into those beautiful emerald eyes. "I came back, didn't I?"

I nod.

"I told you, Harper, you're mine. And maybe I cheated a little bit to get you, but I meant that. I never want to let you go."

He pauses. I feel a 'but' coming on.

"But I have a job to do here, lionfish. I have a job to do."

"What job?"

He cups my face with his hands. They are cool. And reassuring. Like these hands can fix anything. "I know they tell you I'm crazy. And I am. But I'm patient, Harper. And I'm smart. I've outsmarted the most ruthless killers on this planet. I've outsmarted the highest government officials. I've outsmarted drug dealers, and kidnappers, and Admirals, and my mother. I know exactly what I'm doing."

"What are you doing?" I'm breathless listening to him. My heart is beating so fast I'm not sure I can stand up for much longer.

"Killing people, Harper. I'm killing people. Or at the very least… getting them all killed."

"Who? What people?"

He leans down to kiss me again, his tongue probing for more attention. And then he whispers, "Everyone, Harp. I'm gonna kill everyone."

"How?" My legs get weak but James cups my ass and lifts me up, pushing me against the wall.

"Sasha." And then he laughs.

Chills run up my spine. "But you already killed Sasha."

He nuzzles his mouth against my neck and laughs. "Please, Harper. A little faith. I'm a sick asshole, but I have never killed a little girl and I'm not gonna start now."

"I don't understand."

"You don't need to."

"That's not fair, James. I'm not some helpless child. I'm lethal in my own right."

"This isn't your fight, lionfish. This one's mine. So save your moves for something else." And then he kisses my mouth and slaps my ass. "I got this. The only thing I want you to do is let me fuck you. Let me make this world safe for us. And let me keep you forever."

I thread my hands through his hair and breathe him in. "My James."

"My Harper. I want to marry you. I want to take you away. Somewhere safe, and quiet. Somewhere we can get to know each other for real. On our own time. Slowly." He reaches up and brushes a stray strand of hair away from my eyes and tucks it behind my ear. "I want to make love to you under the stars. And sail around the world with you in a boat. I want you all to myself. I'm a stingy, greedy, killer. And I want you. I want to *know* you."

"I want to know you too," I say back, my words so soft they are just barely a whisper. "I've wanted you since the day we turned Six. I didn't understand it, but the way you looked at me, I could feel the love. I could feel your attention." My face begins to get hot and the tears begin to form. "I just want a simple life, James. I don't need a fancy boat or a big house. I don't need money. I just want you. I don't want to be here. I don't want to fight the Company rules and traditions. I just want to run away with you and never look back. "

He swipes a tear away. "I told you we can't do that, lionfish. I told you they'll never let us live. They will find us. I need to take them out."

"It's hopeless."

"It's not." He reaches for me, placing his hand against my cheek. It's cool and feels comforting. I'm warm from the tears and sadness. "I swear, it's not hopeless. Sasha and I have a plan and it will all turn out fine."

I turn my head to look at him and his mouth is there. A slight brush of his lips against mine. I open for him and his tongue flicks in, searching for more contact. Caressing me.

He kisses me for real this time.

There's no hesitation.

Only devouring.

He kisses me like he's the wind. Like he's the sea. Like he's the desert.

He kisses me and he tastes like freedom.

TWENTY-SEVEN

James

Her sweet mouth might break me. Her soft fingers reach for my cock, squeezing it like she's desperate. Her slim hips angle towards me as I press against her. I lift her shirt over her head and relish the blush that forms on her cheeks. Her breasts firm up, her nipples peaking as I look at them. She unbuttons her shorts and lets them fall down her hips until they hit the floor.

"Fuck," is about all I can manage. This girl is perfection.

And then she reaches for the rumpled dress shirt of Vincent's that I'm half wearing. She unbuttons it from the bottom up and then her fingertips brush against my shoulders as she slides the shirt down until that too drops to the floor.

She unbuckles my belt next, letting the two ends fall alongside my hips as she works the button and the zipper of my trousers. A hand reaches inside and wraps around my cock. I tilt my head back and close my eyes. "Put me in your mouth, Harper."

I keep my eyes closed as I feel the soft heat of her breath when she comes closer. The first swipe of her tongue across my tip makes me moan. But when she opens her mouth and allows me to fill her up, pushing my cock to the back of her throat—I lose myself. Fuck.

I grab her head and pump into her. She gags and tries to pull back, but instead of letting her get away, I stop moving so she can recover and keep me in her mouth. "Shhh, my lionfish. Just relax."

She gets it under control and flattens her tongue against my shaft, moaning. The fucking moaning kills me. Her vocal cords vibrate, sending the sensations right to the most sensitive part of my cock.

Her hand cups my balls, kneading them and caressing them, and I take that as her signal that she's ready to proceed. I pump a few more times in her mouth, and then, just before I know she's going to gag, I pull all the way out and squat down to give her a kiss. "I love you."

She kisses me back, her hands greedily reaching for my cock now that it's out of reach.

"I want to make you come, James."

"Baby, I'll come for you any time, any place." I stand back up and put my cock in her mouth.

And this time I take her hard. I fuck her mouth and make her drool. She doesn't hold back. Not one bit. She takes all of me. She takes everything I give her. I press my balls up to her chin and then I come as she swallows me.

When she's done, I take her hand and pull, forcing her to stand. And then I grab her around the thighs and lift her little body up until her pussy is right in front of my face and her legs are draped over my shoulders. She moans just thinking about what I'm going to do. She's dripping wet before I even get started.

I press her back against the wall and lick her, angling her hips so I can get at her pretty little ass. I lap at her clit, flicking it back and forth. And then I drop one leg from my shoulder so I can pump her pussy with my fingers.

"Oh, fuck," she says. "Holy fuck. I'm gonna come, James. I'm—"

Her words make no sense after that. It's just a bunch of noises, coupled with her little hands fisting my hair as she bucks her hips against my face.

When she's slack and quiet I set her feet back on the floor. Her legs are weak, so I take her over to the bed and lay her down on her back as I climb in next to her.

"I want us to run away," she whispers, nuzzling her head into my neck.

Our lovemaking mood is broken, so I just hold her for a moment. "You have to trust me. I can't be responsible for everyone, Harp. But I can be responsible for us."

"Something bad is gonna happen. I feel it. And then I'll be all alone."

"I promise," I say, bringing her hand to my mouth and kissing it. "I promise to live. I promise to be there for you when this is over."

She struggles under my embrace and climbs on top of me. My cock is still hard, but she pumps it a few times to see if I'm still interested.

I am. So I wrap my large hands around her tiny waist and place her on top of me, urging her to begin. She eases down slowly, then lifts up. "I don't believe you. I don't think you should make promises you can't keep. And if you die, James, I will die with you. Even if I live, I will die with you."

"Stop," I chastise her. "I don't want to hear that kind of talk." I play with the blonde strands of hair that are falling down the side of her frowning face. She's not convinced. "I came back for you, didn't I? I promised to come back and I did. And it's only been nine days. I'm early, baby. I over-delivered."

That makes her smile a little and I reach around to cup her ass, lifting her and letting her drop as she slowly rides my cock. Her long hair brushes against my chest and sends chills up my whole body. I fucking love this girl.

"Hold on," I tell her, grabbing her waist again and flipping us over. She spills out onto the sheets beneath me, her legs wrapped around my hips, her arms around my neck. "I want to fuck you from behind."

"I want you to fuck me any way you want."

I lean down and kiss her pretty lips, biting the lower one just enough to make her squeal. And then I rise up on my elbows and knees to give her space to turn. "Face down on the bed, Harper."

She looks me in the eye as she flips, and when her hips are up in the air, and my thick cock is dangling over her ass, I push her legs closed and lie down across her back. My dick squeezes between her cheeks, seeking out her pussy. She gasps when I enter, thrusting hard. I reach in front of her and find her slit, my fingertips rubbing her clit hard. Making her pussy wetter and wetter. Driving her wild and sending her bucking and moaning. I cup my hand around her mouth, forcing her to quiet down, and then I pump my cock into her, over and over, my balls slapping against her wet sex.

When I know she's almost there, I pull her hair. I make her back arch up and her head fall back, her mouth in easy reach.

And I kiss her.

I kiss her hard.

I kiss her like I've never kissed a woman before in my life.

I wrap my hand around her throat and squeeze her chin so there's no possible way for her to stop this kiss.

And then when I feel the walls of her pussy clamping down on my cock, I pound her one last time until I come inside her. Spilling my seed deep in her womb, until I collapse on top of her back, all sweaty and sticky with her sex and her scent.

"Never," I whisper, my eyes closing from the days of travel and work.

Harper squirms under me until I let her out, and then she angles her body into mine, her head resting on my arm, her hands tucked up underneath her chin. "Never what?" she asks sleepily.

"You have always been mine, Harper Tate. You have always been mine and I will never let him have you."

TWENTY-EIGHT

James

The cock of a shotgun stuns me out of my sleep.

"Don't fucking move," the voice whispers, the barrel pressed against my head.

Vincent.

I smile. "I have no plans on moving. I've got her right where I want her." My cock is pressed against her ass, my hand on her breast, her hand gripping mine.

"You're a sick fuck, James."

"Your DNA is the same as mine, brother." Harper squeezes my hand and I know she's awake. "And I hope you know what you're doing with that shotgun. Because you pull that trigger, you splatter both of us. Not just me. So think carefully, Vincent."

He chuckles. "I bet you'd like that, wouldn't you? Take her down with you? Sick. Fuck. Get up."

I remove my hand and Harper withdraws hers without otherwise moving. I ease away and roll out of bed. Vincent backs up several paces as I stand up to my full height. We are eye to eye. We have the same body. The same hair. The same face. The same eyes. But we don't have the same instincts.

I have the instincts of a wild animal.

He has none.

He eyes my nakedness and I laugh. "Like what you see?"

"I'm going to put you down like the dog you are. It's the only death you deserve. Step away from the bed. Don't hide behind an innocent woman."

I put my hands up and walk towards him. He backs up and then pivots so he's got himself between me and Harper.

And then she attacks.

She springs from the bed like a lioness. Her hand wraps around his throat and she squeezes. I grab the gun before the dumbshit pulls the trigger. And then I turn it around and clock him on the head with it. He's already half asphyxiated from Harper's squeezing, so it doesn't take much to knock his ass out.

He crumples to the ground and Harper lets go.

"Jesus," she says, looking at him with what I can only describe as slight disgust. "That was easy."

I grab a tie back from the curtains and bind his hands and then grab my trousers and pull them on. I turn to Harper, who is already dressed. "Watch him for a moment. Let me go look for something to drug him up."

She nods and I let myself out into the hallway. It's quiet up here, but I can hear lots of noises downstairs as preparations are made for the dinner tonight and the party tomorrow.

I ease into Vincent's room and close the door behind me. I hit the bathroom where I know he's got Harper's pills. They're not the best for doping people into unconsciousness, but they will have to do. I grab the little orange bottle and head back to her room.

"He's already moaning," Harper says, when I enter.

"Here, give him ten pills."

"Ten?"

"He's a big guy. We want to make sure."

She takes the bottle and counts out the pills, while I go back to the door and peek out, making sure no one saw me.

"How do we make him swallow them?"

I grab the pills from her outstretched hand and walk over to Vincent. He is waking up, which is good. He's gonna need to swallow them himself once I shove them down his throat. "Get me a toothbrush."

Harper rushes to get that and then comes back, handing it over. I shove it in his mouth to stop him from biting me. "Get me some water." And then I drop each of the tiny white pills into his mouth. When the bitterness hits his tongue, he grimaces and tries to spit them out. But Harper is there with the water and I tip his head back and pour. "Swallow, asshole. Or you're gonna drown. Get me more water, Harper."

"Fuck you," my brother manages past the toothbrush as he spits the water out.

I find two pills and snatch them up so I can dump them back in. "OK, let's do it the hard way, asshole. But I'm warning you. There's worse things than being drugged overnight." And then I lean down into his ear and whisper so Harper can't hear. "I know you kissed her. So believe me, I can think up some very good ways to get even with you for that. Now swallow the fucking pills."

I drop the two pills in and pour the water.

This time he swallows.

"That's a good dog, Vincent. Now, while you drift off into slumber, I'd like you to think about things. I'd like you to think about how they used you, just like they used me. I'm not out to kill you. No one *told* me to kill you. But you're delusional if you think I'm letting you take Harper."

"You're going to get her killed."

"No, I'm the one who will keep her alive. The plan is already in motion, Vincent. It's a done deal. Everyone in this house will be dead tomorrow night."

"If you make it until tomorrow night. No one will mistake you for me, you sick fuck."

"You're wrong. I've been practicing my Vincent routine for months. You think you were watching me? You think you pulled this over on me? Maybe James wasn't ready to see the truth, even as he watched it go down. But I'm Tet, asshole. I see everything."

I untie his feet and pull him up so he's standing. He sways a little when I push him towards one of Harper's closets. She's already got the door open, so I walk him in and kick his legs out from under him, so he crumples back to the ground. Then I tie him back up.

I lean in to whisper again. "You never had a chance." And then I kick him in the teeth. He falls backwards into some hanging dresses, his face obscured by the flowing gowns.

Harper turns off the light and I walk out, closing the door behind me.

"I think he said we're having dinner tonight."

I nod my head and smile at the thought of tonight's dinner. "Yeah. They have a gown for you in his room. I'll go get it so you can get ready." I pull her close and kiss her on the lips. In a familiar way. A way that says I love her and that's all she needs to know right now.

I walk across the hall and go into his closet to find her clothes for the evening. It's been planned for a very long time. Years in the making, in fact.

The gown is a shimmering silver. The skirts are very elaborate and they flow all the way to the floor. It's not very revealing, which is nice. Even though I know all eyes should be on her, I don't want people staring too hard at my Harper.

I choose a suit for me, and change quickly. I add a silver tie and pocket square to match Harper's dress, and choose his most expensive pair of shoes.

My image in the mirror is not Tet.

I sigh at that realization.

It's just James in here after all.

I grab Harper's dress and go back across the hall. She's in the shower, so I lay the gown over a chair and peek my head in. "I can hear people down there, Harp. So don't take too long."

The water shuts off and she opens the glass shower door, showing me her wet body.

"Fuck, woman. Don't tempt me."

"We can skip the party," she says with a smile. Her hair is still dry, but little tendrils of it are falling out all over her face, making her look a little wild.

She drives me wild. "No fucking way. We're not missing this night. Now get dressed."

I back out of the bathroom and make my way back to the hallway. I walk towards the stairs, slowly. Listening for conversation. I hear the Admiral's voice and… Nick.

Harper will be so excited.

I stop at the top of the stairs and listen. I stand there several minutes, absorbing the small talk before the conversation gets heated. I strain to hear.

"No," Nick says. "I'm not taking part in it. I came back to get her. She's not staying here."

"You came back hoping One would be here with the file."

"Won't he?" Nick asks. "You sent him to drug Harper. He killed her, did you know that? He killed her and Tet saved her life."

"Is that a debt you feel the need to pay back?" the Admiral asks him.

I don't hear the answer so I step forward, making a creak on the stairs. Both men come into view and they are looking at me like I caught them in the middle of a secret. Which I might've.

"Well," I say loudly. "Look who's back. It's good to see you, Nicholas."

He tips his head at me. "Vincent."

"Did I hear something about you taking Harper away from me?'

"She's not your prize, Vincent. She's not a commodity to be bought and sold."

"Nicholas," the Admiral snaps.

I put up my hand as I descend the rest of the stairs and cross the polished wood floor where they are standing in front of the floor-to-ceiling windows that look out at the back yard. "Admiral, please. I think I may have a solution that will satisfy everyone."

"What's that?"

"All we have to do is ask her, Nick. She's a grown woman. She's smart enough to make up her own mind. Why do you assume she hates me?"

I stop and watch their reactions.

"She does hate you," Nick finally answers. "She doesn't want this."

"So let's ask her."

"Ask me what?"

The three of us turn our heads up to the voice. She's standing at the top of the stairs in that gorgeous silver gown. Her hair is exactly as it was coming out of the shower. Wispy and unkempt.

She has no makeup on that I can see. I've never seen Harper in makeup. And on her feet are the cutest little silver shoes. She steps down, flashing them at me, making me smile.

"Fucking adorable."

"What?" the Admiral asks, turning to me.

"Your daughter, Admiral. She's so sweet and adorable, I can't stand it." I sigh as she comes down the steps, blushing and smiling.

And then she notices her twin.

"Nick!" Her feet fly down the steps now, and then she runs across the polished wooden floor so fast I'm afraid she'll slip and fall. I almost reach for her as she goes past.

But I come to my senses and let them have their moment.

She flings herself at him. He laughs and all the animosity in the room disappears as he catches her in a hug and swings her around so her dress flares at the bottom.

I might die, that's how fucking cute this girl is.

She peppers her brother with kisses and they talk excitedly for several minutes. "Where have you been? Why did you leave? What were you doing?"

And it hits me at this moment, that these two are talking in some kind of code.

She knows why he left. She knows what he was doing.

And his answers are just as interesting. "All over." "I had business." "Nothing you need to worry about." Because they say nothing and everything at once.

We all know why he left. The better question is, why did he come back?

But it's not the time or place for that question. This is our night.

"You guys were talking when I came downstairs," Harper says, the excitement from seeing Nick still in her eyes. "What were you saying?"

I look at the Admiral. He nods at me.

I take Harper's hand and pull her close. She's too at ease, so I need to put her back on alert. "Harper, you've been with me for several days now. And when I brought you here, you said you would never love me. But I think you'd have to agree that things have developed between us. I think you'd agree that being my promise isn't as bad as you first thought."

"I do enjoy being with you, Vincent."

Jesus, we are playing for keeps right now. It needs to go off perfect. "And it's no secret that we were to be wed. So instead of having the ceremony tomorrow at the party, we thought a nice quiet ceremony tonight would be in order."

She squints her eyes.

"Marry me, Harper. I'm asking you to marry me."

She shakes her head and I almost have a heart attack.

"That's not how you ask a girl to marry you."

Nick and the Admiral chuckle out some *atta girls*, and I nod and drop to one knee. The Admiral hands me a silver velvet ring box and I open it in front of her. "It's your mother's ring, Harper." She looks up at her father and I see tears forming.

"It is," he confirms. "Vincent asked for it yesterday. I keep it in the safe on the yacht. It's the only thing I have left of her. And now it's yours."

I have a little stab of guilt that I'll murder this man tomorrow. But it passes when Harper looks down at me and whispers, "Yes," as she pulls me up off the floor. "Yes."

And then I take her mouth, right there in Vincent's living room.

TWENTY-NINE

Harper

His kiss is so passionate I blush. And when he pulls back and whispers, "I love you," in that soft and tender way that makes me doubt all the stories about the people he's killed, I melt.

He melts me.

He pulls me out of my life and places me in his.

There's a ceremony. Just the three of us and the Company minister attend. I hear the words. I say the words. But the only thing on my mind is James. He is the only thing I see.

The room is massive. The setting extravagant. There are flowers in my hand. A perfect bouquet of short stemmed white roses wrapped in silver ribbon. James holds both my hands in his while the minister talks. He asks us things and we say yes. And then, just before the minister is about to complete the ceremony with a kiss, James puts up a hand and says, "Not so fast." He turns to me and smiles. I am the only thing he sees. "It's not over yet, Harper." I glance at my father and see a look of confusion on his face. But I trust James, so my attention is right back to him. "I waited twelve years for you. I've imagined this moment happening so many ways, but this one," he leans into my ear to whisper, "*lionfish*. This one is the perfect way to end all that waiting."

He pulls back just a few inches, so my father and brother can hear us now too. "I love you. I've always loved you. And I promise you won't regret choosing me."

James. I almost say it, but I stop myself before it slips out. So I lean in, just like he did, and whisper, "You're mine, Fenici. If you go anywhere, I will hunt you down."

He wraps his hand around my neck and pulls me towards him, laughing into my hair.

The minister takes over in our silence and tells James to kiss me.

As if he needed permission.

He kisses me like no man should kiss a girl in front of her father.

He kisses me like a husband.

When that's over, he takes my hand and leads me outside onto the patio. It's bustling with workers setting up for tomorrow, and there's no music, but he draws me close, his hands on my waist as we sway slowly. He brings my head to his chest and breathes a sigh of relief.

"I'm sorry it was such a long wait. I hope this night makes up for time lost. I can't promise you that you'll never fall, Harper. But if you ever need me for anything, I'll be there. I'll catch you. I'll fix it. And if we ever have to be apart, always know that we're together." He lifts my wedding ring to his lips and kisses it. "We met years ago. We drifted apart to become these two people. And now we're back together. One soul, cut in half, reunited."

I'm breathless as the killer they call James declares his love for me. In the backyard of the brother he stole me from, in full view of anyone who cares to watch.

"Did you know Vincent was going to try and marry me tonight?"

He gazes down on me, the light catching his green eyes, making them light up for a moment. "I know everything, Harper Fenici." I smile at that. "I may not always remember everything, but I have it all locked away up here." He taps the side of his head.

"I can't decide if you're a brazen fool, an evil mastermind, or a gentle man."

He grins. "I was foolish enough to believe I could have a woman like you. But my determination paid off. I've had my share of evil moments. But evil begets evil. And the people I killed were doing their share of begetting. As far as a gentle man, well"—he smiles—"only with you, Harper. And our children, when they come."

I rest my head against his chest again, and we dance that way, barely moving, content to be in each other's arms, even if we are in the lion's den. Until finally my feet are tired and I get sleepy. And then he leads me upstairs to my room and we undress each other slowly. He touches my body like he's never touched it before. He worships it. Not sexually, although it turns me on so bad, my nipples perk and my sex throbs.

I touch him too. I search his body for scars. I search his mind for misgivings. But on both accounts, I find none.

No scars. Just a perfect man.

No misgivings. Just his honest love.

And in that moment, I release myself to him completely.

"I am yours, Six."

"And I am yours, Come."

He takes me to bed. I stretch out on the white sheets. Naked. Bare for him. And he worships me in a new way. Our first night as Six and Come is filled with talking and laughing. Touching and loving. And the climax of my night has nothing to do with sex.

He fills me up in a different way now.

He fills me up with love.

The next morning he wakes me slowly with a light touch across my breasts. "It's time, Harper."

We promised each other we would not talk about today until it was really here. And now it is. "I'm listening."

So he talks. And he tells me all about this day before it even starts. He gives very elaborate details. He gives a timeframe and backup options—just in case. He gives me everything I've ever wanted to know about what this day means. What my code means. And what we need to do in order to have a future together.

He gives me hope.

THIRTY

Sasha

"It itches." I scratch the bodice of my fancy dress. It's made up of bunched-up fabric that gathers together in long lines of wrinkles along my torso. Who the hell wears this shit? "And tights? Why the f—"

"Sasha," One snaps. I'm getting on his last nerve, but I don't care. "You said you wanted to do this. You came to me, remember? Do you want to go to the party or not?"

I squint my eyes at him. Merc is suddenly starting to look like a much better option as far as mercenary friends go. "It's *my* party."

"It's Harper's party. You're just there to ruin it."

"Yeah, well…" I got nothing. It's true. I'm just there to fuck it all up. And save Nick. And Harper. But mostly Nick. After we made all those plans about getting the files back, he thinks he can go off and try and do it alone? *I don't think so, buddy.*

"Now," he says, straightening my hair. "What will you say when the Admiral confronts you about being shot on the boat?"

"Sir, my Uncle One—"

"Skip the uncle part, kid."

Asshole. “Sir, One alerted me to Tet’s plan to kill me and brought me a special bulletproof life vest.” I had to cop to that part of James’ plan. Obviously, One needed to know how I survived.

“If he asks anything else, you just defer to me and act like a kid. Just drink some fucking punch and eat cookies.”

Right. I have to control the eye roll.

The car pulls up in the valet area and One and I exit the hotel lobby and get in. The compound is about a thirty-minute drive north, so we have a lot of time to think about what’s happening.

The problem I have is, I don’t know why *he* agreed to this. I leveraged the missing file over his head. The one Merc still has. The one everyone needs in order to make both files work. The one Nick and I would have right now, if this asshole next to me hadn’t drugged Harper and stolen it at the last second. I told One that James has the missing file. I feel bad for James. Using him to lure all the players sucks. But he’s the only one who can handle what I’m sending. He’s the only one who can deals with gang members and assassins. Nick is not experienced enough. Harper is probably useless. And I’m not big enough.

So…

“OK, put on your game face, kid.”

I’ve been wearing my game face since last Christmas when Ford left my grandparents’ ranch.

The car pulls up to the gates of the private community and the driver slides his window down and hands over the paperwork.

It’s not legit. It’s not even an invitation. Why try and fake it? So we decided to just announce who we are and see what happens.

After twenty seconds on the phone inside the gate house, we’re waved through.

The driveway leading up to the main house is flanked on both sides by towering palm trees waving in the wind. There’s so many flowers blooming, the scent of them is almost overwhelming. Almost enough to make me sick.

We’re met by our own little welcoming committee when the car stops. Several men, none of whom have visible weapons, pat us both down. I have a knife strapped to my calf that gets confiscated.

One shoots me a dirty look as we’re escorted inside, but I figure it’s more suspicious to show up with no weapons than it is to get caught with one knife.

This place is packed with people. The sun is just setting, and there's music and that loud rumble of voices you hear in a crowd.

I search for my target.

Nothing.

I see the Admiral. But he's not my target.

I see James' drunk mother. But she's not my target either.

I see… Nick.

And he's holding hands with a dark-haired girl who has the same brilliant green eyes as James.

Nicola. I've never met her before, but I know that's her. Is that the girl Nick was referring to?

I'm just about to make my way over there and start shit when a hand grabs my shoulder. I look up to see the Admiral.

He's not looking at me, though. He's looking at One.

"One. You continue to surprise me," he says, lifting his champagne glass in a fake toast.

"Six is not the only one with surprises," my uncle answers.

"I should say not. Have you come to deliver the file you stole from my daughter?"

"No," One says evenly. "I came to pick one up." I'm still in the Admiral's grasp when they both look down at me. "She's got some very interesting information. It seems that you, Admiral, have been set up by a little girl and her—"

James has One in a headlock and he's choked the words off. "You made a big mistake coming here tonight, One."

"Vincent," the Admiral says with a chuckle. "Please. We're not going to finish this here—" And then he must look James in the eyes, because the realization of who he is flashes across his face.

James snaps One's neck and is easing him down to the ground before anyone actually realizes what just happened. In fact, only the few people closest to the Admiral understand. I'm just about to search One for the file while everyone is distracted by James when I see my target being pulled out of the room.

I leave the ballroom just as the room erupts in panic and follow Harper and her would-be abductor down the west wing of the palatial mansion. She's pulled through the door, not fighting or crying out, either. So that alarms me. What if Harper is working for someone else as well? It seems we are nothing but a clusterfuck of double and triple crossings tonight.

I stop at the closed door to the room they entered and then open it a crack to see what's going on.

THIRTY-ONE

Harper

"Let go of my hand, you bitch." I yank my arm out of her grasp and turn, my ridiculous full skirts on this elaborate gown swirling at my feet in a whoosh.

"Where is he?" Mrs. Fenici spits. Her breath is laced with alcohol and her hands are trembling as she points her finger in my face. I smack it away and she tries to grab me again, the bangle bracelets on her frail wrist jangling. "That is not my son out there. Where is my son?"

"That *is* your son, you drunken bitch." And then I look over at the door and spy Sasha. I want to smile and give her a hug but she looks like she's all business. The witch turns to follow my gaze and Sasha gives her a little wave.

"Hello there, Mrs F. Do you need help, Harper?" she says in her sweetest little-girl voice.

I almost smile. "No, thank you, Sasha. I've got this. Why don't you go find Nick and take care of *his* little problem."

"Will do," she quips, and exits through the door just as quietly as she came in.

"What are you doing? I demand to see my son. Who did you marry last night?"

"Not the son you think," I say in a low voice. "And you're not going to leave this room, I'm afraid. So you won't be seeing anyone."

"Right," she spits through her teeth. "I'm—"

"You're sick," I say, cutting her off. "What kind of mother sends her sons off to kill? What kind of mother sends her daughter off to kill?"

"Your James did that."

"No." I shake my head. "My James owed your assassin a life debt. He had no choice. You're the one responsible for all this because you were so power-hungry or weak-minded, you didn't have the wherewithal to resist selling out your children." She opens her mouth to speak, but I slap her so hard across her mouth she sways sideways and falls to the ground.

"You bitch," she seethes.

I step forward and kick her in the teeth with my pretty white shoe that matches my pretty white dress. Her head crashes back against the floor this time, her legs sprawled out in front of her.

I lean down and grab her dark hair and look her in her green eyes as I yank her head back. "It's unfortunate that I never learned to shoot, because then you'd go quickly. But the only weapons I have at the moment are my hands. So I'm going to take your life with those."

She thrashes her legs and waves her arms around, trying to land a punch, I think. But this woman, Jesus. It's almost like a lioness toying with a mouse. She is weak and pathetic. I dodge her attempts, but even the couple that land don't hurt bad enough to make me wince.

And then I have a fleeting thought. Why? Why am I such a highly trained killer?

She sees this change in me and smiles.

"He set you up too, darling. Just like I set up James. You've been programmed, dear. You've been programmed to kill, just like all the other Company contracts."

Contracts. "What are you talking about?"

"You're here to kill me, darling. Going through with it only brings you farther into the fold. Why do you think we pay such close attention to Company children, Harper? Because we love them? Please," she laughs. "Please. I've been told you're naive, but surely you understand what you are? What you were born to be? You're a killer, Miss Tate. One of the secret ones. One of the Zeros brought up in a loving family. But a killer nonetheless. *He* called us all here to die by your hands, just like last summer on the ship. Your father is the evil one in this world."

"Then why come?"

"Because I have someone here representing me as well. And your father should know better than to double-cross me. We both have daughters, Harper. And mine is killing your brother. Right now. But she's not the only delegate I brought to this party, sweetie. Your father and I talked about joining forces. Becoming one powerful family by wedding you and Vincent. Our last hope for a compromise. But then… you killed my delegates. And they let you get away. Your father protected you, even smoothed things over with Vincent. But I knew better." She reaches up to tap her head just like James did last night. "I know everything."

When she echoes his words I panic.

"And his secret mission—the one he's been on for years but has no clue about—is to kill everyone at this party, Harper. James didn't come up with this plan, dear. I did. And you walked right into it. You—"

I snap her neck just as easily as James snapped One's and then I let her drop to the floor and go searching through the desk until I find what I need to finish my job here tonight.

A gun.

And I guess she's right.

I'm a goddamned killer.

But at least I'm not a goddamned liar.

Because she's full of shit. I don't believe he's been programmed. I know my James is damaged, but he's not a ridiculous robot programmed to kill.

He kills of his own free will, or not at all.

THIRTY-TWO

Sasha

The entire mansion is in an uproar. People are screaming while the Admiral's voice booms through the downstairs, asking people to remain calm.

Good luck with that. I chuckle as I make my way down the hallway. Several people look at me funny, but I'm not so out of place that they stop to question me. I'm sure there's no kids allowed at this thing. But I almost look grown up in my fancy dress. I try to walk calmly as I look for Nick, but I'm not used to the fancy shoes, and that makes walking difficult.

I look in each room as I pass, and then finally decide Nick is not on the ground floor. I look up at the second floor, consider it, and then nix that idea. If he's not around, then he got the files off One while James was busy dealing with the aftermath. So that means he's outside heading towards the rendezvous point.

I scoot past the lingering crowd as the Admiral assures everyone that Vincent just had a moment of rage over… blah, blah, blah. Lie, lie, lie. He has to know that was James.

So I just tune that shit out. James is a big boy. If any of us can take care of themselves, it's him. I check my watch to see how long I have.

Three minutes.

Once I get past the people outside, I kick my shoes off and run. I know where Nick's going and I bet I know who Harper was referring to when she mentioned his little problem. I run my fastest all the way down the path that leads to the marina, my feet pounding on the stone path. I take the steps two at a time, making my stupid dress poof up each time I land. And I'm only halfway there when I see them arguing on the dock.

This place is quiet. It's just a small marina to begin with, but tonight it's dead. No one is down here but us.

I creep up as close as I dare, and just barely catch the conversation when she yells.

"You're not leaving me, Nicholas. There's no way you're going to take what you came for and walk away from this promise."

Oh, boy. I got a live one. I sneak down the stairs one at a time, so they can't detect me. I'm a good stalker. I've hunted wild animals my whole life. I know how to creep up on them. And this Nicola is definitely one of the wild ones. When I reach the sand, I slip under the stairs and crawl towards them.

She's trying to grab for Nick, but he keeps slapping her hands away. "Stop it," he growls at her after she tries to slap him. "I'm not anyone's promise, OK? So stop begging. It's sad."

"It's called loyalty, Nick." She's practically foaming at the mouth, that's how pissed off she is. "You should want to be loyal to me. You promised you'd leave Sasha and marry me."

"You're delusional. I never said that shit. You're insane, just like your brothers. You're an assassin, Nicola. We don't get promises."

"Liar!" she screams. "You're a liar. I know you were promised to Sasha. And I'm gonna kill that little—"

Nick grabs her by the throat, but she's already in attack mode. Her body spins, her foot comes up, and she's about to connect with his face when he grabs her by the ankle and flips her over and throws her down on the hard dock with a crash. She winces, but gets back up to fight again.

I'm done with this shit. Nicola's taking time with Nick that belongs to me. I hike my skirt up and pull the knife from its sheath, tucked into the waistband of my tights. “He said that’s enough.”

She backs up and whirls to face me. “Ha! Your little child bride is here to save you, Nick? Are you skills really that bad, Eleven?”

“I’m not here to save him, you dumb bitch. I’m here to *kill* you.”

“Right—”

The knife sticks her right in the throat. She makes a gurgling sound and clutches at the blade. But it’s useless. I hit an artery. She falls to the ground choking on her own blood.

I look at Nick’s face for a clue to how he’s gonna take this. “I usually warn them that I don’t miss, but she never gave me a chance.” And then I offer a small smile.

“What the fuck are you doing here?” He doesn’t reciprocate the smile.

“One had that file, Nick. So I’m here saving the day. I brought him here.”

“Do you have it?” he asks, hope in his voice.

“You have it!”

“I don’t fucking have it! That’s what we were just arguing about. She didn’t believe me. James has it.”

“James.” Jesus Christ. Can this mission get any more complicated? I look down at my watch, but I don’t need the time to know that the slaughter has already started. I can hear the AK’s and screaming from the beach. And now we need to go back up there.

I grab Nick’s arm as he pushes past me, heading for the stairs. “Don’t go.”

“What?” he asks, barely turning to face me. “What the fuck are you talking about, Sash? Harper’s up there!”

“James can take care of Harper, Nick. Just don’t go. This is our chance to get out. To get away. Let the gangs take out the Company. James will get Harper out and meet Merc here in a few minutes. We can get another boat and leave. Let them mess with the files. We don’t need the stupid files.”

But the whole time I’m talking, he’s shaking his head. “We need those files more than you know, Sasha. We can’t leave here without them. I can’t leave here without Harper. You stay here, wait for Merc. I’ll go get Harp and James, and we’ll be right back.”

"No!" I stomp my bare foot. "No. I'm tired of always being put last. Why can't you put me first for once? You say you love me, that you'd do anything for me. Then choose me, Nick. Choose me and let's go!"

I push him in the chest and he grabs my wrists and holds them tight. "I did put you first, Sasha. I left you in that hotel and told you to move on. Get a life. Live it. I put you first and you came here looking for me. With this crazy fucking plan that Tet cooked up and you bought like it was on sale for Christmas. What do you think is happening here right now? You can't plan a job like this and then go half in. You can't leave your team behind. That's bullshit."

"I don't care! I just want us to live. I just want us to get away and live our lives."

"There is no *us*, Sasha. How do I fucking make you understand? I'm not taking you as a promise. We're not killing all these people tonight so I can take you as a promise. When we get out of this mess, you're going home with James. Not me. So stay here and stay out of sight. Or come with me and be prepared to fight."

And with that, he drops my wrists and starts jogging back towards the stairs.

What choice do I have?

I follow him into the war zone, hoping and praying we get to leave here together, but knowing damn well we're probably all going to die.

Because isn't that how James and I planned it? Isn't that what we decided? Shoot everyone. That was the original plan Tet told me outside the Hummer that day in the Wal-Mart parking lot after Harper was drugged. *We'll shoot everyone.* And this party, a party he knew was coming for months, was the perfect place to accomplish that objective.

No one left alive.

And when your army is a street gang who've been looking for revenge for a dozen years, well, all bets are off about who lives and who dies when the bullets start flying.

THIRTY-THREE

James

I laugh one of those maniacal laughs you only see in movies. I know Harper left with my mother and Sasha followed as planned. So I've got a few minutes before all hell breaks loose to have some fun.

"Vincent?" the Admiral asks.

I shake my head. "Wrong." I watch him come to terms with the fact that I spent last night with his daughter. Hell, I married her—even though it's not legal, it was still a ceremony of promise and commitment. And he not only watched, but gave me his blessing. "Sorry, Vincent couldn't join us tonight. He's not feeling well. Something about seafood poisoning."

The Admiral's face goes white.

"Seriously?" I ask, taking a step toward him. "You of all people should be able to recognize me by now." I take him by the neck, just like I did One, and have his back up against my chest before security shows up. The little red laser dots flash across the Admiral's white shirt.

"Don't shoot," he tells his men.

"We can take him out, sir," one kiss-ass says. His laser sight flashes me in the eye.

I press my gun to the fleshy part of the Admiral's lower back.

"For fuck's sake, lower that laser before you piss him off and he shoots me for fun."

"Oh," I say, backing up so I can have a wall behind me. "It's already been tons of fun, Admiral. Twelve years of good fucking times, right? You thought you'd what? Just keep giving me orders and I'd just keep following them until you decided I wasn't worth your time anymore?"

He doesn't answer, so I press the gun into his kidneys to help him along.

"No," he groans. "I treated you like a son."

"Yeah," I say with an ironic laugh. "You sure did treat me just like my father did. But don't worry, Admiral, you won't get the same fate. Because you won't be brought back from the dead like him. I'll finish the job and end it right."

I spot Sasha running outside in a crowd who figure it's best to get as far away from me as they possibly can, and breathe a sigh of relief. Harper must be safe and my mother must be dead.

I check my watch. Three minutes. Harper appears in the room and people give her a wide berth as she approaches.

The Admiral laughs. "There she is." He says it with some relief as Harper raises her arm, a gun in her hand.

My eyebrows go up as she walks up to us. At first I think she's aiming for me, but I realize it's not me, it's him. Her father.

"Harper," he says. "Do your job, honey."

"What's my job, Daddy?" she asks sweetly.

"Protect me at all costs. Kill Tet. Kill anyone who threatens us."

"Is this part of that brainwashing you did on me?"

Fuck.

"Because I have to tell you." She lowers the aim of her gun and I can actually feel the Admiral let out a breath. But that's before she shoots him in the leg. "It didn't take."

I have to shake my head, because that bullet was so close to me, I feel the impact in my own body.

"Oops," she says, as the Admiral wails in pain. I let him fall forward onto the ground and take out two security guards.

The whole room erupts in screaming and then the bullets start spraying. A woman standing next to me is shot in the torso and blood splatters me in the face.

They're early.

Lesson learned. Never fucking trust a gang member to do *their* job on *your* time.

I grab Harper's wrist and pull her down to the floor in front of her father so I can keep her safe and relieve her of the gun. "Get the file from One, Harp."

She crawls over her father's wounded leg and begins searching One when the Admiral pulls a gun out from his pocket and aims it at me.

"Really?" Tet takes over. He grabs him by the neck just as a shot comes from the gun. Plaster from the ceiling showers down on us, but I don't even notice when a large chunk crashes on top of my arm.

Because when I have a man's neck in my grasp, there's only one way that shit's gonna end.

Even over the rapid firing of AK's, I hear the crack.

His head goes limp. His body relaxes. And when I look at Harper, she smiles. "We're free."

"Not yet, lionfish. Now we gotta get the fuck out of here."

The entire ballroom is chaos. People are running, they don't' last long, because the bullets are flying. So the runners fall, littering the floor with blood and bodies.

"Crawl with me, harp." I get down low and make our way to a banquet table. I lift up the tablecloth, but there are several people under there already. "Out," I hiss at them, pointing Harper's gun.

They do run, but I grab two of them by the arms and yank them backwards. I pull Harper up as they bolt, and we run with them. Between them.

A living shield.

A woman goes down in front of me, then a man behind. But we book it. The people outside are coming in and the people inside are going out as mass confusion ensues. There's bodies and blood. People trip, fall, and then get trampled. I pull Harper through the French doors and head for the beach. There's some Company people running the same direction in front of us, but I shoot them and they go down. Another small group is in front of them, but as soon as they hear the shots, they dart off the path to the beach and head for the trees. Sasha's army will have to take them out.

Just as we get to the stairs, I see Nick and Sasha.

"We're gonna make it," Harper says.

And there's a split second where I really think we might. I almost let myself hope. I almost give in to the happy ending.

But that's when Mistake Number One from my time in Honduras steps out from behind Nick, a gun to his side. Sasha is being held as well. They've got a hand over her mouth, making it hard for her to breathe.

"Tet," the deformed Nicaraguan leader laughs. "My pet, Tet! The little girl promised my men you would be here. I admit, I had my doubts. It's been a long quest, my faithful enemy, but finally, a fruitful one."

He's got a red scarf wrapped around his head so you can't see the part of his face I blew off twelve years ago. He looks every bit his age. His dark skin is wrinkled and worn. The tattoos on his face, a mark that separates them from some of the other gangs, are fading, they are so old. But he lives. He still lives.

He laughs. And his evil movie-star laugh is enough to give me the chills.

I have not seen him since I was rescued by One. I have not laid eyes on him since that final day in captivity. Even when I was down in San Pedro Sula, I never had the urge to seek him out.

Because I'll be honest here. That motherfucker scares the shit out of me.

"My men gave the little girl my word." He nods to Sasha's captors and they release her with a shove that makes her fall forward on the ground. "And my word is good, even when dealing with the Company." Now he looks at Nick and Nick is pushed forward too, but he does not stumble. "And her." He points to Harper and I have a moment of panic.

"Hey." I divert his attention from Harper. "I just killed One for you. The Admiral as well. She," I say, nodding to Harper, "killed my mother. The leadership is dead."

And that's when another shadow emerges from the darkness. "Not quite," Vincent says.

THIRTY-FOUR

Harper

Vincent steps forward, looking a mess from his two-day Ativan coma. His gaze is on me and for some reason, I can't stop looking at him. It's such a mind-fuck for him and James to be identical.

"Harper," he says.

"Take one fucking step towards her," James growls, "and I will snap your fucking neck."

The disfigured gang leader laughs as his men come towards James and I expect a huge fight to break out right then, but he doesn't fight back when they grab him by the arms. He shoots me a look as they tug him from my side, and then he looks over at the leader. "Just let them go. I'll come with you, but just let the girls go. And let Nick Tate get them to safety."

"James," I say. But my desperate whisper isn't even loud enough for him to hear.

Sasha is pushed forward and she runs to me, clinging to my waist.

We're gonna let this end like this? We're four killers. Trained assassins. Surely we can at least put up a fight?

The men walk James to the leader's feet and then push him down on his knees. He looks up at the ugly man and smiles. "Let them go, Matias. Let them go and I won't finish what I started twelve years ago."

Matias kicks James in the stomach, making him double over. "Fuck you, *perro mascota*. My new pet dog." He squats down so he can look James in the eye and then he presses the barrel of his gun to James' temple. "You're not in any position to negotiate. And if you say one more word, I kill those girls right now." He smiles to reveal only half a mouth of teeth. "And make you watch."

Then he straightens up and takes his attention to Nick. "Let's walk down to the beach so I can have time to consider my options." He waves a hand and his entourage starts shoving us towards the steps. James is pushed forward and he begins the descent first, but he's surrounded by Matias' security, so I can't even see him. Sasha and I hold hands on the way down. She's trembling. For all our bravado, we're not seasoned in these kinds of confrontations. Not like Nick and James are.

I'm terrified. I feel like one of us is about to be murdered, and that is most likely James.

When we finally make it to the sand, Sasha and I are pushed off to one side while Nick and James are lined up in front of the ocean. The tide is high, there's very little beach left at the moment. And I have a brief moment of anxiety as I worry about the water crashing us against the rocky cliff that is only a few yards away.

"Shoot them both," Vincent says. "Just shoot them. I gave them to you, now let me take the Tate girl and leave."

"Shut up, *cabrón*. No one is leaving yet."

Sasha hugs me tight, and then she leans into my ear and whispers. "James has the file, Harper. If they take James, they take the files."

"Where the fuck is that guy James said was waiting with a boat?" But as soon as the words are out of my mouth, I see the boat lights in the small harbor. It's motoring towards us as a very slow rate. Everyone turns to look, but then the engine cuts and it drifts over to the dock and bumps up against it.

"Your ride?" the gang leader asks me.

I nod. The Hispanic man walks towards us and stops right in front of Sasha. To her credit, she meets his gaze. "We made a deal," he says. "You gave me what you promised, so I will give you what I promised. Go."

"Nick too," Sasha demands. "I asked for Nick and I'm not leaving without him."

"Take him," Matias says with a laugh. "I have the only man I came for." And then he looks over at James. "Since One is already dead, my new dog, you will pay for his sins instead."

Sasha grabs my wrist, but I can't move. I cannot leave here without James. There's no fucking way I'm walking off this beach and leaving him here.

I pull away from Sasha and—

"Harper," James says, from down the beach. "Harper, stop. Listen to me."

I shake my head and back away from the ugly man and Sasha. "I'm not part of this deal."

"You're damn right you're not part of this deal. She's coming with me, Matias." Vincent walks forward like he's gonna take me away, but Matias aims at the ground in front of his feet and shoots. The sand flies up in his face, making a cloud of dust.

"Someone shut this asshole up."

They go for him, but Vincent is big and he pushes the first guy out of the way. They start fighting, but Vincent breaks away, and the last thing I see is him running into the ocean and diving into a crashing wave.

"Shoot him!" Matias calls. "He's no one. Just a copy of the man here on his knees."

A few men run along the water shooting into the waves, but it's dark and I don't see anything.

A shot rings out, hitting the cliff behind Matias, and then all four of us have guns to our heads.

A voice comes over a speaker from the boat still banging against the dock.

"Fenici party of four, your table is ready."

Sasha snorts, but then the little red laser dot appears on James' chest. "Let him go, Matias," the voice in the boat says. "Or I'll shoot him right now. And if you make me shoot my friend, I'm gonna shoot you next, motherfucker."

"Shoot him!" Matias calls. "It's a mercy killing. Because we're going to set him on fire. Right here on this beach." A man approaches from the stairs carrying two cans of gasoline and Matias walks over to meet him, his arms outstretched.

"See how efficient we are?" He stops and looks back at James, who is strangely calm for a man whose fate involves going up in flames in a haze of accelerant. "But don't worry, dog. I'm not going to kill you, *cabrón*. I'm going to makes sure you live to feel the pain, just like you did me." He points to another man who is holding a fire extinguisher. "I don't want you to die, dog. That's too easy. I'm going to make sure you live to feel the humiliation at being disfigured."

"Stop," I shout. "Just stop. This is not happening. You are not doing that." I point to Matias. "I won't let you."

"You won't let me?" He walks forward, pushing Sasha out of the way as he approaches and then he grabs me by my hair. I twist under his arm and spin around his back, my hands ready to clamp down on his throat, when a shot rings out at my feet.

Matias pushes me to the ground and then smacks me in the face.

"That's enough, Matias," James says. "Touch her again and I take someone out. Let her go and you can do whatever you want with me. But you're gonna let her go first."

"As if you can negotiate," Matias spits.

James smiles. I can see it even in this dim moonlight. "You know I can, motherfucker. You know I can. I'm playing ball with you right now because these girls are here. But you hurt one of them, and I've got no reason to be compliant. So let them go. Let Nick Tate walk them up the dock so that boat can take them away. And I'm yours."

"No," I say from the ground at Matias' feet. "James, I'm not leaving here without you."

"Take her away, Nick." James looks at my brother and they stare hard into each other's eyes.

Sasha stands in front of me and offers her hand. I accept and she helps me to my feet. "Let's *go*, Harper. Before he changes his mind."

But I shake off her grip and walk towards my new husband instead. There's protests in Spanish from the gang members, and probably Matias himself, ordering me to stop. But I don't stop. I walk right up to James and wrap my arms around his neck. "I'm not leaving you here. I'm not. I refuse to leave here without you. I can't live. I told you, I can't live. I'd rather die than live without you."

His hands wrap around my neck and he threads his fingers into my hair as he pulls me tight to his chest. "I love you." And then he sighs.

"Wait," Nick says off to my right. "Wait, Matias. I have another option for you."

I don't want hear the option. I really don't want to hear the option. Because I know what he's going to say, just by the tone of his voice.

"Take me instead."

Sasha screams. "No! No! That was not our deal!"

Matias laughs, looks at James one more time, then my brother. He's considering the options. He's considering who Nick is. How he might help him.

"I have information, Matias," Nick says quickly. "Information James does not. Information that you will want." Sasha is still screaming and there are several men holding her back from running up to ruin this deal. Nick's voice is strained. "The Company isn't dead, only subdued. I can get you all their assets. I can offer you resources you will never get on your own. I can give you more power than you've ever dreamed of. Just let James go. Let him take my sister and the little girl. And don't ever look for them again."

Everyone goes silent. Even Sasha stops her wailing to wait for the answer. I count the number of times the waves crash as the deformed man stares down my brother.

Does he want a way forward into the future? Or does he want revenge for the past?

He walks over to James and stands a few paces off and laughs. "I'll tell you what. You apologize to me. On your knees. For what you did. And I'll consider this deal."

James shakes his head and gets to his feet. He walks towards the gang leader, his hands in the air. "Jesus fucking Christ, Matias.

It was a job. OK? A fucking. Job. It was never personal. I didn't kill your family. Hell, I didn't even kill *you.* I missed motherfucker. Why do you fucking think that is?" James stops right in front of Matias and I wait for the shot. I wait for the retaliation and the vengeance that will take his life. Take him from me forever. "Did you ever, after all this time, ask yourself why I fucking *missed* Matias? Did it ever fucking occur to you? Did it ever cross that pea-brain of yours that I missed on purpose?"

What?

Matias shakes his head and laughs. "You want to face me, after all this time, and say what you did was merciful?"

"Dude, I was a kid. In a fucking war zone. Your brothers strung me up. I never even got to talk to you about it. You never came to me after you recovered and asked about it."

"You were a spy."

"And you *knew* I was a spy. You knew because I told you back then and it's pretty clear now, I don't work for these people. I work for me. I told you everything I knew before the shit went down. It's not my fucking fault you didn't listen. And now you *know*. You've known since that day twelve years ago. I was telling the truth. And the last time I was down in San Pedro Sula, I stayed clear, asshole. Out of respect. You never saw me. You never heard my name. They never knew I was there."

Matias stares at James. "We knew someone was there."

"No one ever said my name. They never said my name because I never told them who I was. I did my job, which did not involve your gang, and left. It's a fucking. Job. Matias. And you know the biggest difference between you assholes down there and the Company? They always knew it was business. You take everything personal. You never see the big picture. You let your emotions run your gang. For once in your fucking life, think about your bottom line."

I look at Sasha and she shakes her head. She did not know they had some sort of business relationship. But am I surprised? James always said he worked for himself. And right now, that seems to be true. Because he's been cheating against the Company since he stated playing the game.

"Matias," Nick says, interrupting whatever is going on between these two killers. "Look man, you can kill James if you want, but I'll have my sniper in the boat shoot you at the same time. And you'll never walk out of here. Or, you can make a deal. You can take me. Leave James and take me and shit gets real easy, real fast."

Matias stares at Nick for a few seconds. Then back to James. I don't know what the two men are thinking, but somehow, some way, they come to some silent agreement. "Done," Matias says "Take them now, before I change my mind."

Sasha is wailing again, but James grabs my hand and tugs me along to collect her. "Shut up, Sasha," he growls at her once he's got a hold of her arm. And we are dragged from that beach. Me looking back at my brother. Sasha looking back at her promise. We are dragged all the way down to the very edge of the dock where James' friend Merc waits in the boat. He's still got the rifle trained on the gang members. But they are climbing the stairs.

Sasha is crying as she gets into the boat. "Why? Why did you do that?" She flings herself at James, pounding on his chest. "I hate you! I hate you!"

I should hate him too. I should hate James for choosing himself over Nick.

But that's not what happened here.

Nick offered himself up for a reason. Several reasons, actually.

Me.

Sasha.

All of us Company kids.

Nick did the only thing he could.

Because James is the one who has the file, not him. James is the one who had to live, even if all the rest of us died.

Or everything we've done over the past year—the death, the struggle, the sacrifice, the pain—along with all the information on those two discs—would be lost to a vile street gang who would have no idea what to do with it if Nick didn't get James out of there.

So I hold Sasha instead. I hold her tight and whisper soothing things in her ear. "They won't kill him, Sasha. They won't hurt him either. He will survive. He will survive and so will we."

"He's gone, Harper. He's gone." I know she wants to say more, but the sobbing takes over and she can't.

There's nothing more to say, anyway.

He's just gone.

THIRTY-FIVE

Sasha
One week later
Rock Springs, Wyoming

I look around the hotel room and the sadness is overwhelming. I can't deal. I can't deal at all. I have lost everything I've ever loved to bad people. My mother, who I never even met. My father. My grandparents. And now Nick. My last thread of hope that life would be worth living after all this was done.

But it's not worth living.

It fucking sucks.

My chin starts to quiver and the tears begin to fall. Again. I've done nothing but cry since we got here to the hotel room a few days ago. Harper and James are staying in here with me. Against my wishes. I wanted to be alone, but James refused.

Today is the last paid day for this room. The last chance for Nick to come back to me.

And it's almost noon now, past checkout time.

So…

Reality.

It sucks.

James walks through the open door and stands there, a black

figure, backlit by the morning sun. "You ready, Smurf?"

I shake my head and sit on the bed, staring at the dirty hotel carpet. "No," I whisper. "No."

"He's not coming here, Sasha."

"I know." I swallow down that rock in my throat, but I can't seem to make it go away. "But I don't want to leave."

James takes a long breath and sits down on the bed next to me. "I'm sorry."

"I know." He's been apologizing for a week now. I'm sorta sick of it.

"But Merc sent me a message a little bit ago. He thinks he's finally figured out how to get the files to open."

I sniff and look up at my friend. "What's on them?"

"Secret money accounts, mostly. Names of all the Company members, of course."

"Huh. All that bullshit for money and names? It's hardly worth it."

"Yeah, but it's the non-money stuff you're gonna wanna hear about."

"Oh, God, no. I'm not interested." They've been talking about the 'programming' I was subjected to by my father. I'm having a hard time coming to terms with Nick being gone, I really don't need to know that my father was brainwashing me to kill people when I got older.

"We still think it's on there, Sash."

Hearing James call me Sash makes me let out a sob. "Only Nick called me Sash. So don't."

James takes a deep breath and lets it out. "OK. But that brainwashing stuff might be true, so you need to be aware of it."

"Consider me aware."

"We're ready to hit the road now, so where should we go? You get to choose."

"I'm not going."

"Sasha, don't press me," James growls. "I get it. You're broken right now. But you're not gonna stay broken forever. You gotta let that shit heal. And today is the day you start, Smurf. I brought you here so you'd see for yourself. Nick is not coming back, OK? He's not coming back. He made a deal with that cartel and he's gonna see it through. And you are thirteen years old. You can't just wish yourself grown up and start a life with a man who really is. He's not gonna come back and bring you into that life, Sasha. He's not gonna take a child bride. Everything he stands for is against what you want him to be. So let him go. Let him make his way in the world. He let you go so you can make yours. Don't give up. He'd never give up if you were the one who sacrificed yourself to give him a second chance. He stayed behind for you. So you'd get that information off that disc. Information your father put on there. Information you need."

"I know all this."

"Then snap the fuck out of it, Sasha. He's not dead, OK?" I don't respond, so James lifts my chin and forces me to look at him. "He's not dead."

I shake off his hand and continue looking down at the carpet. "I know he's not dead. And—" I let out another sob. "And that's even worse, James." I look up at him as the tears stream down my face. He tisks his tongue at me and lets out a sigh. "It's worse because that means he *chose* to leave me." And then I can't hold it in anymore. I just cover my face with my hands and cry.

James leans over and pulls me into a hug. I wrap my arms around his waist and press my tears into his soft t-shirt.

"I'm sorry, Sasha. I really am. I know you love him. I know you thought you'd have that happily ever after with him. But it was never meant to be, kid. It wasn't."

"It's not fair," I whine. "It's not fair that you get Harper and I get no one."

"You got both of us, Sobby Smurf. You made out like a bandit. And besides, I didn't get Harper right away. I had to wait twelve years. She was too young when I fell in love with her. So that's one reason why Nick had to leave, Sash. He fell in love with you and you're too young. He'd be a very bad guy if he didn't walk away, you have to understand that."

I have nothing to say to that. I know it's true, but I don't want to admit it. I don't want this to be my reality.

"So, Harp and I were thinking. We'd sorta like to go see all that dinosaur stuff you talked about back in the desert. We're close to Thermopolis. We looked that dinosaur place up online. Did you know they were voted number one dinosaur museum in the whole country?"

"Duh," I say. "I've been to Thermopolis dozens of times."

"Well, we haven't. It's only like three hours away, kid. What better way to spend a summer afternoon than driving up to see some dinosaurs?"

I look at him. He's trying so hard to be here for me. To help me.

"Right?" he asks again.

I nod out a yes. "I suppose. You guys really don't know enough about dinosaurs." I sniff away my leftover sobs. "History is something you should understand, you know."

"I really should, Smurf. I need you, kid."

I look up at him and the tears are back.

He leans down and presses his head to mine. "I do, Sasha Cherlin. I need you. I can't lose you to this sadness. You have to snap out of it. We're gonna take our time, OK? We're gonna take things slow. Go on road trips. See the West from the window of a truck. Just… relax and be normal for a few months before we decide what to do. OK? Sound good?"

I nod again. And then we stand up and walk towards the door.

I take one last look around the room. I remember Nick, lying on the bed next to me. Telling me these same things.

I give up one last sob for what could have been, and walk out.

James closes the door behind us.

And that's it.

It's over.

THIRTY-SIX

James

Six Months Later
Medicine Wheel National Historic Landmark
Bighorn National Forest
Wyoming

"Oh my God, I'm freezing!"

"Wimp," I say to Harper as we climb the hill that leads to the medicine wheel monument. Sasha is way out ahead, halfway up the hill already.

"Why in the hell did we wait until December to come to this place?" Harper asks as she hugs herself.

It is damn cold up here. Negative two. But we're all dressed for it. We've got the best winter gear money can buy. Merc finally cracked the financial accounts on those files, so there was a windfall payday for all four of us. We didn't find the brainwashing stuff—not yet, anyway. And maybe it was all a lie. Maybe they just told us that shit to scare us. Or make us do things. Who knows. But if it was on that disc, it's very well-hidden.

"Brr," Harp complains again. I know Harper is not that cold, she's just got an aversion to it. She was excited to see snow the first time, and then she was ready to hit the tropics. But we're still doing the Dino Smurf tour of the West. So…

"It's the Winter Solstice, Harper. It's like a big deal or

something."

"No," she laughs. "The Summer Solstice is a big deal. The Winter Solstice is something no one in Wyoming gives a crap about. It's dark at four o'clock. It's freezing. And it's just… *wrong*."

"Hey, you know what?"

"What?" she asks as we continue to climb.

"It's almost sundown. So we can hang out and watch the sunset."

"No, thank you," she laughs. "I'm all about one quick look at this wheel thing, then we're out of here."

When we finally get to the top Sasha is just standing there, looking over at the fenced-in area where the wheel is. Should be.

"You can't see it," she says, disappointed. "The snow is covering it all up."

"Fuck." I'm such a loser. I never even thought about the snow covering up the rocks.

"You can see some of them, Sash," Harper says. "Look, there's the tip of one."

The medicine wheel is a wheel made out of rocks placed in the ground hundreds of years ago by the native people in this area. It's pretty crooked and if you ask me, you have to use your imagination on the best of days to see a wheel. But even crooked squiggly lines of rocks are better than no rocks.

"But you can't see the spokes," Sasha says. "I knew it was stupid to come."

She was supposed to come here with her father for the last Summer Solstice. But we were hiding out at Merc's desert house that night. And her father was dead. So yeah, that trip was canceled.

And then she said she never wanted to come see it. We've driven by this national forest dozens of times in the past six months hunting dinosaurs. But she refused to stop.

Until I offered to bring her for the Winter Solstice.

"Let's go," Sasha says, turning around to head back down the hill to the truck. "I'm done."

"Wait," I say, grabbing her jacket as she passes me. "We can make our own spokes. Look." I walk over to the fence and step over it. The snow is so high along the fence, that's easy to do. And then I walk out to the center of the circle and lie down in the snow. "Come here, girls. We'll make our own spokes and watch the sunset."

I expect Harper to be the first to groan, but she surprises me. "Come on, Sasha. We won't let a little snow ruin our trip." She walks out to me and positions herself a little to the left, with her head touching mine. And then she pats the ground on her left. "Here's your spot, Sasha! Come on."

Sasha's boots crunch along in the snow as she walks out towards us in silence. She takes her place on Harper's left and my right. Her head touches both of ours, and she lets out a sigh. "Now what?"

"Now," Harper says. "We watch the sunset. And wait for the stars."

The mountains are so high up this way, the sun is already behind them, but the light hasn't yet faded. We're in the perfect moment of dusk. When the air is not yet black from night, but still has that hazy blue-grey of in-between.

We've watched hundreds of sunsets over the past six months. Not every night. We forget sometimes. But almost every night.

That moment passes quickly and then the night is upon us.

We lie there, three spokes in a wheel, for several minutes before Harper's mittened hand points to the sky. "There," she says. "You can't see Orion in the summer. So if you came here on a summer night instead, you'd miss him."

Sasha asks questions about the stars and Harper answers them. She tells stories of sailing the seas looking up at the sky to know where they were heading. She tells stories of the constellations and the myths behind them.

And Sasha listens with the ear of a girl deeply interested in these things. A girl who needs more than just one long road-trip as her formal education.

This is the moment I decide that my Smurf can't stay with us anymore. She can't lose the childhood the Company stole from her.

This is the moment I realize, maybe for the first time in my life, that what I'm doing is wrong.

Thirty-Seven

Ford

Christmas Eve - Fort Collins, CO

I pace the length of the front room of our house, staring down at my minions. The face-eaters, as Spencer and Veronica affectionately call them, are lined up in front of the Christmas tree. The blinking lights reflect in their brown eyes.

We have three highly trained protection dogs now that Five is here. I look across the open space first floor of our historic bungalow in Fort Collins, and spy Veronica cuddling Five to her chest as Ashleigh hovers over her, talking a mile a minute about our baby. Veronica's swollen belly, ready to deliver in just a few more weeks, provides a convenient place for little Five to rest his tiny bootied feet.

I smile at Ashleigh when I catch her looking at me and she smiles back, rocking a fussy one-year-old Kate to her chest. And then I take my attention back to business.

"Face-eaters," I say. The term has caught on. They are collectively called that now. "Let's go through the rules one more time." I turn on my heel and pace in front of them. "One. You will not drool on her. Two. Licking is by invitation only." I look at Jimmy for this. He's our newest addition, purchased once we found out Ash was pregnant with Five. His ears prick up when he notices my attention. He's a licker, so naturally, he objects to that one. "Three. No sniffing of—"

"They're here!" Rook calls out from the couch in front of the window. I think she's more excited than anyone. She jumps up and stands in front of me. "Are you ready?"

I nod at her. "I was just making sure the minions are on their best behavior."

Rook straightens my tie and then pats me on the shoulder like I need moral support.

I kinda do need moral support. This new addition to my family is a big deal.

My daughter, Kate, came to me through my wife, Ashleigh. My son, Five, is ours together. So Sasha is more mine than ours at the moment. I feel the need to do this right. To bring her into the fold properly.

The doorbell rings and everyone stops talking for a moment. I look back at them and see nothing but smiles. They are excited, but they go back to what they were doing and let me handle it. Spencer and Ronin are sitting at the kitchen table, drinking beer and laughing about something. Ash and Veronica are still busy with Five and Kate. And my mother is talking to Mr. Li with a little too much interest.

"You're gonna be fine, Ford. Just answer the door," Rook says.

I nod and walk over to the front door. I can see him through the small window.

James Fenici is coming to my house for Christmas Eve dinner. And he's bringing me a kid. Not just any kid. Sasha Cherlin. The girl who started… well, I look around one more time before reaching for the door handle… everything. She started everything.

I open the door and Fenici smiles and extends his hand. "Aston."

"James," I say politely as I shake. And then I look down at his young wife and wish they were *all* staying. Rook would love to have a friend who is actually younger than her for once. "You must be Harper." I shake her hand too and move aside to let them in.

But it's the girl who's missing who makes my heart skip a beat.

"Where is Sasha?"

"In the truck," James says. "She's having a hard time. She said she'll be in soon. But you know, she's thirteen. So…" He shrugs.

I grab my coat and put it on. And then I gently place Sasha's present in the box Ashleigh prepared. It's a red box with a green bow. And the bow stays on, even if you open the box. Ashleigh says all the best presents have bows attached to the tops.

I take her word on that.

"Be right back," I tell my houseguests. And then I walk outside and pull the door closed behind me. Sasha looks out the window of the black truck and I give her a small wave.

She does not wave back.

I take a seat on the top step of my porch stoop. It's cold tonight, but not too bad. We can wait her out.

It takes her exactly two minutes and seven seconds to decide to come meet me on the porch. And as she walks up the path to my home, I take her in for the first time since I met her last year.

She doesn't smile, but I know the braces are long gone. Removed before her grandparents died. But her hair is long and flowing down her front. And she's tall too. Much taller than the little girl I met last Christmas Eve. She's wearing a fancy black coat with fuzzy mittens and hat to match. Her dress is a dark red, as are her shoes. She even has a purse that she clutches in her hands as she walks towards me and then stops at the bottom step.

"Hi, Ford." It comes out fine, but a moment later, she's crying. She takes off her mitten and wipes her eyes. "I'm sorry."

"You don't need to be sorry," I tell her back. "It's a hard thing to do to leave the people you love."

She nods her head but the tears stream down her cheeks. "I don't know what you want from me. James says I have to learn to be a normal teenager. But I'm just not sure I can be that person." She sniffs and wipes her tears again. "I don't want to disappoint you, Ford. Because if you left me, or dropped me off somewhere…" She shakes her head and more tears fall down her face.

"That's not what James is doing, Sasha. He's not dropping you off. He's bringing you home. To me."

She removes her other mitten and drops them both on the ground so she can wipe her eyes. I grab her present, then stand up and walk down the stairs, picking her mittens up for her, before sitting back down on a lower step. "You wanna know what's new for me this year?" I grab her hand and tug a little. Just enough to get her to step forward and then sit down on the step next to me.

"Sure," she says, hugging her coat close to keep warm.

"Last year when we met, I had no girlfriend, remember?"

That makes her smile and nod. "You were so clueless."

"And you were so smart. I owe you big for the lessons I learned from you, Sasha. Because this year, I have a wife, two children, and another on the way." She looks up at me, surprised. "No. You, Sasha. You're the one on the way."

"Oh." She tucks her hands into her pockets and takes a deep breath. "I don't know what you want from me. I'm not a good candidate for a daughter. I don't really follow directions. And I'm opinionated and not willing to bend." She looks up at me. "I'm kinda stuck in my ways and my ways are keeping me stuck. Does that make sense?"

"Sure. It makes sense. I'm not expecting you to act a certain way. I just want you to find yourself, Sasha. Find the girl you want to be, instead of the girl you left behind, as Rook would say."

"Rook, the girl-who-is-a-friend?"

"Yeah." I laugh. "Rook. She's inside waiting for you. So is everyone else. My mother. Ashleigh's father. My friends and children. We're all here for you, kid. I told you I don't celebrate Christmas. But now I have kids. So I do. And I don't have parties, either. But today you came, so I felt a celebration was in order."

She stares up at me with those blue eyes. "What if they don't like the girl I am now? What if I can't find the girl I want to be fast enough for them to like me? I've killed people, Ford. I've seen things. I've lost so much." She starts crying again. "And I'm angry. OK? There. I said it. I'm pissed off because this life sucks. And I always get screwed over. And just when I get attached to James and Harper and think, OK, this is my family, then they don't want me anymore."

"They love you enough to accept the fact that they can't give you what you need, Sasha. And we can."

"You guys want me to go to school. And be normal. But I'm not normal. I'm a really fucked-up kid." She looks over at me. "A really fucked-up person, Ford. I'm probably not even safe to be around other kids my age."

"Don't be silly. And besides, I start filming in New Zealand for that show I'm producing. We leave in a few weeks. So you won't even go to school this year. We're gonna go bum around Down Under for six months. Enjoy two summers. Get to know each other. And then next fall, we'll come home and be a normal family. So we have three whole seasons to practice."

She's silent after that. And we just sit in the cold saying nothing for several minutes. "What's in the box?" she finally asks, her curiosity getting the best of her.

I pick it up and place it on her lap.

"What is it?" Her face turns up to mine when she feels the shuffling inside. And then she laughs and lifts the lid off.

The little gray kitten is just stretching out her paws inside the blanket. "Oh my God," Sasha says. "A kitten. I've never had a kitten."

"I wanted another dog, but Ashleigh, pfftt." I hike my thumb behind me in the direction of the house. "She put her foot down on that one. We have three face-eaters. So I figured it was fine to get something cuddly." She lifts up the kitten and brings it to her chest. "For you."

She nuzzles the kitten's soft fur and smiles. Her shoulders relax. My heart swells with her change in behavior. That a kitten can do this for a sad and broken child, well. It's touching. "Merry Christmas," I say.

She snuggles the kitten once more, and then takes a deep breath. Like maybe she can do this after all. "Merry Christmas, Ford."

I stand up and offer her my hand.

She accepts it.

And then we walk up the front stairs to her new home together.

I stop at the front door and turn to her. "You're officially part of the Team now, Cherlin. But first things first. I need you to hate Ronin. No matter how charming he is, you must not fall for it. He may be on the Team too, but we're mortal enemies till the end."

"Got it," she says, laughing, as I open the door and wave her inside.

She walks into the room and everyone greets her while I stand back and take off my coat and hang it up in the closet.

I watch my friends and family as they fuss over her like I told them to. She never had a chance against Ronin's charms, but that pretend indifference gives us something to plot about. Making Ronin miserable is good times.

Sasha greets everyone and shows James and Harper her kitten. I can physically detect the moment when James sighs with relief.

Not because he's getting rid of her, as Sasha thinks.

But because she's getting a second chance at a normal life.

Last Christmas Eve I was sad. I was sad that Rook didn't want me in the way I wanted her. I was sad that the women I thought were fulfilling a need for me really weren't. And I was sad that I let my life become so meaningless after my father died.

And that night, Rook told me she changed her life by wishing on a star the year before. She went from a sad abused girl to a strong and confident woman. In one year.

So I tried it. I was desperate. Like Sasha is probably desperate for change tonight too.

Never in a million years would I have thought that wishing on a Christmas star could get me *this*. So I look out the window real quick and find Sirius, our gift-giver.

And I make a wish for Sasha this year.

I wish her heart to be mended.

Maybe it doesn't happen in one year. That's OK. We are patient people. I will be there for her as long as she needs me.

Just please, I ask the star. *Make her whole again.*

Epilogue One

Harper

"What's wrong?" James asks as we snuggle together on Harrison's new plane. James gave him a fat bonus for putting up with him all these years. The new plane is nice. And much bigger than the last one.

"Just..." I don't know how to say it so he's not offended. "Those girls at the party. Rook, Ronnie, and Ashleigh. I like them."

"They like you," he says, playing with my hair. "And they like Sasha. She's lucky."

"So lucky. I'm gonna miss her. And I'm gonna miss them too. Even though I just met them tonight, that Rook, she told me a story about her life that... just wow. They all told me stories about themselves. And Ashleigh's Kate. She's a Company kid, but they didn't seem to know that. They never mentioned any Company business. What if—"

"They won't, Harp. She's gonna be OK. Sasha will keep an eye out for her. And Merc is close by. Kate will be OK."

"Buckle up, kids. We're landing," Harrison says over the speakers.

"I'd like to live in a town like that, James. And have friends like that."

"One day, Harper. We'll go back. But for now, we deserve some time alone. Don't you think?"

I smile as I sit up and buckle in to get ready for the landing. "Tell me about it again, James. I'm lost in the dream of small town family and friends. So tell me again what we're doing."

"We're starting over, lionfish. Two people, one life. We've got sixty foot sailboat in Miami. Just waiting for us to set her loose in the Caribbean."

I picture it. I picture sailing through paradise with my husband. I don't think about *before* anymore. I did at first, back when things were still raw and the memory of that night still fresh. My hear hurt for Nick.

But I let it go. I let him go. He wanted to take that path in life, and it's not up to me to stop him.

And James is right. Now that Sasha has a new life, we deserve one too.

"We'll spend every day in the sun," he says softly as the landing gear detracts and our new life gets close. "And every night we'll watch it set. We'll explore beaches, and reefs, and each other. We'll sail across the ocean in the spring and be in Australia for the summer solstice. We'll see Sasha and her new family then. We'll see how much happier Sasha is. How she's moved on. And then we'll sail back. Or find new places to explore. And when we get tired of that. Or bored. We'll start talking about the future. Long term plans, Harp. Babies and houses and best friend kind of stuff. When we're ready to settle, we'll carve that life out for ourselves when it's time. But don't rush it. Don't be too eager to get the happy ending, Harper. Because getting there is the fun part."

"Yeah," I agree as the plane touches down. "It's the journey that counts. Not the destination."

"Unless the destination is bed. With you."

I press my face into his neck and take him in. He might be crazy. And he's definitely dangerous. But I like him this way. And I can't think of a single regret for how we got to be in this moment right now.

Harrison taxies down the runway as I look out the window at

Florida. After we stop, and Harrison's crew opens the jet to let us out, James has to lower his trademark shades down his face.

Because we walk right out into the sunset.

EPILOGUE TWO

Sasha

Ten years later

Denver International Airport

"Miss Aston?" The man is tall, wearing a dark suit, and has the look that screams government.

And suddenly, ten years of manners and settling are washed away. "Who's asking?"

"I'm Special Agent Jax, Miss Aston. And I have a few questions for you. Please come with me."

"Am I under arrest for something?" Fuck. He leads me through a set of double doors, and then another door, and then another door, until I'm three layers deep inside the fucking Denver International Airport. We finally come to a small office, where he waves me in and says, "Please, take a seat."

I take my seat. *Just be cooperative, Sasha*, Ford tells me in my head. We've covered my tracks well since he adopted me ten years ago. But we've always planned for the day when people discover my history is a lie.

"Am I under arrest?" I ask again.

"No, ma'am," he says. "I just need to ask you some questions, if that's OK."

"What if it's not OK? What if I want to call my dad?"

He sits down at the table opposite me and opens up a folder. "You are Sasha Aston, correct?"

"You know I am. I just got off that plane. So I was checked in."

"You came from…"

"Peru." I fill in the blank for him.

"What was your business in Peru, might I ask?"

"I was at an archeological dig. They found bones."

"Bones?"

"Dinosaur bones. I'm a paleontologist. Well, a grad student. It was a summer internship. Why?"

He looks at me for a moment. "Impressive. And your father is Rutherford Aston IV?"

"Yes." I swallow hard. Jesus Christ, we are totally busted for something. "I need to know what's going on. You're scaring me. Did something happen to my dad?"

"No, ma'am."

"Stop calling me ma'am. I'm twenty-four and you look like you're about thirty."

He eyes me down the bridge of his nose. "Thirty? I don't look thirty. I'm twenty-seven."

"What?" I have to shake my head at that. "What do you want, Special Agent Jax? If I'm not under arrest, then I'm leaving."

He flips the page in the folder just as I stand up, and produces a photograph that steals all my breath away.

"Do you know this man, Miss Aston? Can you identify him for us?"

I shake my head as I study Nick's face. His perfect face. The blond hair, the brown eyes. The steely gaze. I can picture him smiling at me in that hotel room in Rock Springs. *Live your life*, he told me. "Never seen him before," I say, lying right to Special Agent Jax's face. "Why?"

"Take another look, Miss Aston. How about this one?"

This time, Nick is shirtless. His whole body is covered in tattoos. His chest, his arms, his neck. And when I look closely, even his hands have tattoos on them.

I shake my head again. "No, sir. Sorry."

"Hmmm," Jax says. "Well, that's interesting, Miss Aston. Or

should I call you Miss Cherlin?"

I stare him in the eyes and do not flinch. I don't deny or confirm. From this point on, I do not talk. I say nothing until I'm given a phone and then I call my dad and tell him I need Ronin. Ronin, the liar. Ronin, the one who talks for all the Team members if we get in trouble. Ronin. That's the only name on my mind right now.

"They call him Santino down in Central America. But here in the US, they call him Holy Boy. He's white with blonde hair—but somehow, he's the second highest-ranking member of the *Mara Perro*, Gang of the Dogs."

"Very interesting. But what's this have to do with me?" Shit, I just broke the no-talking rule.

"That's what I'm trying to figure out, Miss Cherlin. If that's who you are, it makes a lot more sense."

"How so?"

"I think you know how so." He grins at me and flashes a dimple. His eyes are a dark blue color and his hair is light. Not quite blond, but not quite brown, either. He's handsome. That's probably why they sent him to me. Thinking I'm easily distracted by a pretty face.

"I don't have time for this. I don't know that man—"

"He knows you, Miss Aston. He knows you very well. Because he's sent more than two dozen people here to find you while you've been digging down in Peru this summer."

"What?"

"Did you two have some unfinished business? Before you took on this new identity?" *I can't breathe.* "Or some prearranged agreement to meet up in the future?"

I shake my head no. "We didn't."

"But you do know him?"

I just gave myself away. I lean on the desk and bow my head to try to think clearly. Agent Jax places his hand on mine.

"Miss Aston, I'm not here to arrest you or pry into your past. I understand your fear right now, I do. Better than most. But if you know him, and if he's looking for you, you should understand... he's probably planning on kidnapping you."

"*What*?"

"We've intercepted several of these men he's sent to look for you. Three of them confessed to this plot. Now I don't expect you to tell me much. Just yes or no. Is this man, the one they call Santino, Nicholas Tate?"

I nod. "That's him. I'd recognize him anywhere. But I haven't seen him in ten years. I don't know anything about this stuff. I was in Peru, not Central America—"

"You're not under suspicion, Miss Aston."

"Then why did you ask me here?"

"We don't want to arrest you, Sasha. We want to recruit you."

END OF BOOK SHIT

I started this book thinking...

...there was never going to be another book about these people once I was done. But obviously I've changed my mind. Jana, my assistant, wanted a Sasha and Nick book so bad. But I couldn't see it before I wrote the end. I really didn't expect to write that second epilogue until I was there, just typing away. But I like it. Sasha will have another book.

But the next book about these characters belongs to Merc. He gets two books, in fact. One should release in late February or early March and the second one should release a month later. That should be it for him, but what do I know? Maybe I have some big idea when I write the end of that one too.

But the next book on my publishing schedule is called Three, Two, One and it releases in January. I can't say too much about it because I'm not writing it yet. But it's different than anything I've done before. It's another suspense and it will definitely be erotic romance. Look for a cover reveal in mid-January and if you want to help me spread the word about it when it releases (and win prizes like gift cards and signed books while you're at it) sign up for the release day share list here.

My year is winding down and Coming For You is the last book I'm going to publish in 2014. I think it's fitting that I started and ended this year with Ford. His book, TAUT, was the first book I released last January. And even though I have like twenty-four books to my name now, TAUT is still my favorite. I had the best time writing that book. Sometimes I just want to open it up and start reading, that's how much I still love it. And writing Ford is so simple. It's like, man, I just *get* that guy. He's so much fun.

I'm not making any promises, but I'm not gonna deny that I don't have these characters (like all of them) possibly involved in Sasha's book in some way. But we'll see. I don't like to be too predictable, so you won't find that in her story. But I think I can tell you a tale about what they've been doing for ten years and make it sexy and interesting at the same time.

This is probably a very boring EOBS for you guys. Sorry! I'm just ready to relax for the holidays and run some sales in December. So keep an eye out or better yet, sign up for my newsletter and never miss out on a sale or a release day event.

Thanks for reading. Thanks for loving James, Harper, and Sasha. And thanks for leaving a review on Amazon! Cause I KNOW you will, right! :)

Julie

Made in the USA
Middletown, DE
13 January 2017